P9-CCN-007

Dear Justin and Ryan

Hitch your wagons to God and He will keep you safe in the palms of His great and mighty hands - all the days of your life.

C. E. Johnson

Aug 2017

Warriors
of the
Light

TERRIFIED TOURIST

C. E. JOHNSON

WESTBOW
PRESS®
A DIVISION OF THOMAS NELSON
& ZONDERVAN

Copyright © 2017 C. E. Johnson.

All rights reserved. No part of this book may be used or reproduced by any means, graphic, electronic, or mechanical, including photocopying, recording, taping or by any information storage retrieval system without the written permission of the author except in the case of brief quotations embodied in critical articles and reviews.

This is a work of fiction. All of the characters, names, incidents, organizations, and dialogue in this novel are either the products of the author's imagination or are used fictitiously.

Interior Art Credit: Karl Hebron

WestBow Press books may be ordered through booksellers or by contacting:

WestBow Press
A Division of Thomas Nelson & Zondervan
1663 Liberty Drive
Bloomington, IN 47403
www.westbowpress.com
1 (866) 928-1240

Because of the dynamic nature of the Internet, any web addresses or links contained in this book may have changed since publication and may no longer be valid. The views expressed in this work are solely those of the author and do not necessarily reflect the views of the publisher, and the publisher hereby disclaims any responsibility for them.

ISBN: 978-1-5127-8092-5 (sc)
ISBN: 978-1-5127-8093-2 (hc)
ISBN: 978-1-5127-8091-8 (e)

Library of Congress Control Number: 2017904694

Print information available on the last page.

WestBow Press rev. date: 7/12/2017

Table of Contents

The Inside Intel

J. K. Rowling created a brilliant group of characters that use external power to problem solve in an otherwise ordinary world. In *Warriors of the Light*, Karah Klark, the heroine does the opposite. She enters an unfathomable world in the cosmos filled with combatant-type creatures and demons and uses God's real power that comes from within to conquer them all.

As Karah and her comrades trek through God's secret Kingdom of Khalee just beneath the surface everyone understands they're being served-up lessons of faith and learning how God operates. They experience their own courage and character grow into the kind they can use to slay real world dragons and bullies on planet Earth - Now, that's more than miraculous!

If Harry Potter was to meet Karah he would be happy she would introduce him to her companions, but he might want to avoid the Demoness in Training. He would be amazed by how she triumphs over evil without a cute magic wand or uttering a single magic spell. He would quickly learn that his make-believe-magic is no match for God's real, tangible power.

Karah is an inspiring example of growth by trial and error. She's proof to kids that it's okay to fail as long as they pick themselves up and keep trying. She's an ever-changing scrapper tomboy one moment and an enchanting girlygirl the next. She's up. She's down. She's smart. She's naive. She freaks out then pushes through. She's easily discouraged, but never ceases to be strong and courageous. She's real, never perfect!

Children relate to Karah and watch her blossom on every page knowing it's because God loves her and she loves Him. They understand that she and God are determined for her to fulfill her God given purpose which is to draw children to Him and for His glory teach them how to face challenges that scare them and threaten their daily lives.

Chapter One

AN "IT" A "HIDEOUS IT"

'CHING-CHING! CHING-CHING!' DREADDOG's mind rang up dollar signs when a strange woman offered her a colossal stack-of-cash for the young girl sleeping in the backseat of her car as if she represented many pulls on a slot machine. As a pathetic reason for her inexcusable dealings came to mind she peered at slumbering Karah and said, "You would have agreed to sell yourself if you'd seen the satanic look in that woman's eyes."

Removing a sweaty hand from the steering wheel she reached over her shoulder to lock the door. Catching a glimpse of herself in the side mirror she felt a piercing stab-of-shame. *"Some 'Top Watchdog for Children' you are,"* she mused. *"Reporters don't know about your frenzied gambling binges. You are aptly nicknamed Dreaded-Dreaddog by the children you're supposed to protect."*

Sudden full-force rain began drumming heavily on the roof of her car. No longer vacillating between guilt and hoped-for winnings at the Golden Palm Casino, Dreaddog leaned forward and looked out her windshield. Taking in the site of heavily sagging clouds barreling overhead like dams ready to burst she hoped Karah was a child who could sleep through anything.

When the strange woman drove up behind her and revved her engine, urging her to depart for the location where the deed was to be done, Dreaddog recognized her vehicle and the purplish clouds of engine smog it was coughing up. *"It's the fuming van that followed me off the hospital grounds this morning,"* she reflected.

Thinking she had no choice, Dreaddog started her car and pulled out of the all night diner parking lot wishing she'd never stopped for a cup of coffee. When she entered the rural highway heading east she recalled seeing the woman in the corridors of the hospital's mental health wing. Her mind fast forwarded to the same grim set jaw pressing against the glass partition of the nurse's station while Karah said her goodbyes. She envisioned her a third time writhing and withering like a nocturnal SheDevil creature in front of brightly flashing cameras. *"Cameras taking pictures of the only member of a family that didn't die in an explosion caused by an oily residue sent to NASA for analysis,"* she realized.

Foamy spittle formed on her lips and her pimples seemingly started popping on their own as she explored reasons why only a child psychologist who lived in an undisclosed location could speak with Karah about whatever she might have seen just before she stopped to put a pipe in her snowman's mouth that subzero morning.

Dreaddog checked her rearview mirror again and was simultaneously shocked and relieved to discover that the SheDevil's van and vapor trail were gone. Relief burst from her beefy belly and she loosened her grip on the steering wheel. Before long she could see mile marker 13 approaching. Pressing hard on the accelerator she planned to propel past it, but as if the rest stop had plans of its own the day instantly became night and it drew her car in like a magnet. Her spineless fear escalated as she realized her life might also be in jeopardy.

Unaware that she was about to be sold like a china doll at a flea market Karah awakened as the car rolled to a stop.

Wanting to get the release part over so she could make a fast getaway Dreaddog said, "Time to go potty, Karah. Come on. Get up. Get out of the car."

Karah's dulled senses remained unchanged as she fixed her eyes on a streetlamp positioned at the edge of the sidewalk leading to a broken-down tourist office. She'd lost her ability to respond the morning her family's ashes drifted from the sky and gathered in her glazed, ginger hair. Her eyes slid slowly to the left, but only after lightning struck through the night leaving trailing splinters of quickly dissolving light. Nothing inside her wanted to move and she had no need to 'go and do' the baby word Dreaddog told her to 'go do.' Adrift and aloof, she remained fastened in place.

"You need to go potty," Dreaddog said, again. "Get out of the car."

Still and expressionless Karah stared back at her so-called-protector thinking, *"When I have to go I'll be the first to know."*

Dreaddog's lips formed a grim curvature as she absorbed Karah's inaction. Knowing she needed to get her out of the car, and fast, she heaved her flabby arms over the seat. Sensing Dreaddog's heightened anxiety and fearing what she might do next Karah opened the car door. Having no raincoat, she hesitated as the angry storm stripped leaves off thrashing trees clawing at the night air. Losing the little patience she had left Dreaddog pushed her out of the car and closed the door behind her.

Karah stiffened and sent Dreaddog a hard look for only giving her a cement block outhouse to turn to for shelter. The distance also alarmed her - It was far from the parking lot. She became even more confused when Dreaddog locked the door as if a voice on the radio had just said: 'We interrupt this program to bring you a special bogeyman-on-the-loose alert.'

While imagining filthy, fat rats lurking inside the bathroom she succumbed to a howling gust of wind seemingly trying to scoop her off the sidewalk. Even a paper heart that surrendered its middle to a branch rushing past her feet represented some sort of threat. Gripping her sweater across her chest she took off running. As lightning struck, shrieking birds burst out of a cluster of giant pines. She looked up wishing she, too, had wings and could fly herself to some safe place.

When she reached the entrance she was thankful something didn't come screaming toward her with lethal purpose and shove a child-sized body bag over her head. She put her hand through the doorway and carefully worked it up and down the wall feeling for a light switch. As she flipped it to the on position the bulb burst. In that moment, only Dreaddog's car horn proved to function properly when it sent her a 'Get going' honk.

"Just go in and pretend," she told herself. *"Hang around long enough for Her-Dreadediness to think you had the nerve to go near a disgusting public potty pot."*

Finding motivation in her words, Karah took one weary, step inside. Smelling something more foul than pukey toilets connected to rusted pipes she pinched her nose and circled in the dark. Scratching stirring sounds arose brewing up haunting affects. The mental strain of every footstep, no matter how carefully placed, was too much for her to bear. Her panic peaked. She bolted out of the bathroom and into SheDevil's plot to sweep her into an evil net.

Having an inexplicable Good Samaritan moment, Dreaddog turned her high beam headlights on thinking Karah might be able to escape if she caused SheDevil pain and anguish the way flashing cameras did at the hospital. Her headlights exploded.

Feral terror turned the brown in Karah's eyes white as she was grabbed from behind and shards of glass flew toward her. She threw a thrashing, kicking, screaming, fit using her hands and feet and elbows and knees as weapons but she had no impact on her abductor. Her screams rose an octave when she caught a glimpse of her captor's reflection in a puddle and saw burning sparks appear in a woman's face as if a spell-ish disguise was wearing off.

Once hurled into a van that didn't have the words *Child Protection Services* painted on the side she flung herself at a dirty window and plastered her fists and forehead on it. From there she could see Dreaddog behind the steering wheel of her car with her head dangling by the crook of her neck and a deep wound on her forehead just below her hairline.

There was no one who could save her at rest stop mile marker 13 on Highway 495. The only presence besides the SheDevil's was malicious rain slicing hard at her reflection in the glass.

Feeling jagged edges of the ripped vinyl seat stabbing at the fleshy backs of her legs, Karah looked at what stepped into the van and said, "What are you? What are you going to do to me?"

SheDevil's response was silence. She merely dabbed at a cut on her chin.

"I hope I hurt you, you, you, you're not a you," Karah said. "You're an IT. A HIDEOUS IT."

A toxic odor permeated the air as SheDevil turned in the driver's seat and smiled.

Karah froze as the sulfuric stench coated her lungs. What was sneering at her didn't just crawl out of a swamp.

"So much for happily ever after," SheDevil said.

As the van's engine backfired and the wheels began rolling out of the parking lot Karah's desperation and confusion welded together causing her to sink into her seat praying for her life. The storm ended in that moment and the moon began illuminating her with its brightness, but darkness continued filling her mind like a deadly plague.

She embraced ill fainted thoughts telling her she was going to detonate like her family until the vision of a woman riding a great white stallion with iron pounding hooves appeared in her mind. While the vision galloped nearer and nearer and each pounding hoof came closer still she convinced herself that HIDEOUS IT's master plan was to trample her brains into pancake-size.

She got on the floor with her arms folded over her head and screamed, "GOD HELP ME!" To her astonishment a rich voice whispered, "Will I do?" in her ear. Her jaw plummeted when she tearfully peeked through her bangs and saw a throbbing shadow reach for her hand. She didn't want to, but she slowly accepted the gesture and went *whoosh* then *poof.*

Chapter Two

EYES LIKE SWIMMING POOLS

NEARLY BOLTING OUT of her tightly buckled shoes Karah ran when she saw a chance to escape from the tomb she found herself in. She wasn't fast enough. The archway went *whoosh* then *poof* and a wall appeared in its place with three women wearing costumes painted on it. She screamed as before, "GOD HELP ME!" This time no help arrived. No Spiderman. No Superman. Not even a wished for Mighty Underdog swiftly pawing its way under the wall.

Her next thoughts were altogether unexpected. She recalled her grandmother tucking her into bed and saying the Children's Bedtime Prayer with her. Tears cut a path through the dirt on her cheeks as she recalled the words: *"Now I lay me down to sleep. I pray the Lord my soul to keep. If I should die before I wake, I pray the Lord my soul to take."*

With her fisted knuckles turning white she recited the prayer over and over - Each time with greater force - Clinging to it like a life preserver in a violent wind tossed sea. As she did, long forgotten memories of her grandmother soared into her consciousness. She pictured her angelic eyes and reflected upon how they would sit outside in the moonlight on long, hot summer nights talking about whatever was on their minds. As she recalled one special night she remembered the moon shining so bright they could see someone watching them from behind a tree in the distance.

Wanting to speak with Isabella, the Angel of Well-Everything, Jesus appeared next to her in the viewing room of the monastery where Karah was temporarily stashed. "I, too, was troubled knowing what was going to happen," He said, "but she did need to get a taste of the Devil and get her wits scared out of her. Maybe now she'll listen to Divine instruction."

"Isabella," God said from afar, "I instructed you to bring Karah here because My children on Earth asked me to teach their children how to fight spiritual warfare. We're going to teach Karah how so she can return to Earth and be the answer to those prayers. As you know, Satan wants to destroy her so that can't happen. She's now in your subjects' collective protective custody because she needs the kind of training only the Citizens of Khalee can provide."

"When she finds out why she's been brought here," Isabella said, "there'll be no holding her down and I can't keep her against her will. What am I supposed to do when she screams, 'I wanna go home. I don't want to be a spiritual anything that Satan is after?'"

A smile appeared on Jesus' face as He turned Isabella to face Him. "As always, I will direct when and how truths are revealed," He said. "During this season of Karah's life I will be her Master Teacher. She will find out what she needs to know from Me. For now I only want her to know me as Rabboni, her Master Teacher. Make sure everyone knows. You're to be like a mother to her. She's going to need you, especially after I tell her what will be asked of her."

"Allow me a word of warning, Isabella," God interjected. "One of many strengths I've given Karah is the ability to dissolve even your resolve. Strengths she needs in order to become who she will become, but strengths that will work against her until she learns to let Me channel her."

"Firm minded as always I will be," Isabella said.

"The first thing she needs is reassurance and some light-hearted fun," Jesus said. "Dazzle her. Give her everything her heart desires for 24-hours."

Karah suddenly and inexplicably smelled the alluring fragrance of her Grandmother's perfume. Fully expecting to see her the heavy wet lashes that shadowed her cheeks flew up and her eyes swiveled wildly out of control. She was still alone, but her cave-like chamber was transforming into a fantasy paradise. Her beaming face dangled with animation as her eyes landed on the shoebox-shaped slab of granite she'd been sleeping on. It was now gold with a majestic angel figure beset on each end bowing with unfurled wings. She backed away as glorious statues arose silently out of the sand surrounding it.

"Either my eyes are playing tricks on me or my dream is coming true," she said.

Things happened so quickly Karah's mind tumbled, but once the springing up of things stopped her wits took hold. She was more than just a little thrilled to be in what now looked like a King's palace complete with a King's ransom. She exploded with joy and began shoving her fingers into magnificently carved urns with stringed jewels and pearls spilling over the rims.

While adorning herself like Cleopatra familiar sounds and delicious aromas seized her hungry senses. She ran for a gold gilded dragon creating chocolate covered popcorn in its crystal belly. Just sure it was hers to enjoy while playing the starring role in a fantasy action movie she stuffed fistfulls of the candy-coated treats into her mouth.

The dragon machine's ruby eyes looked like they were going to burst into flames and its pulsating nostrils took a swift sniff of her as a saintly statue draped with layers of luxurious silk broke its pose and walked toward her. When the splendidly figured statuette bowed a bowl of fruit with a spigot spouting fruit juice appeared in its arms. A silver goblet simultaneously materialized in Karah's cupped hands and began filling with the much needed refreshment. The saintly sculpture then straightened its back and turned stiff.

"I must be dreaming," Karah said. "Somebody pinch me."

In response to her request to be pinched something with sharp claws scurried up her leg and hopped and skipped from her chest to her chin. She fell in love with the precious creature bedazzled with glowing gems and jewels as it settled on her nose and looked into her right eye. Now knowing she wasn't dreaming, she plucked what she thought was a lizard off her nose and the babbling began:

"How'd you get here?" she said as she caressed him with her cheek. "Oh, you're probably wondering how I got here. I can't answer that. I wish I could. You're sooo cute. My name is Karah. I will call you Spot. I named my cat Blossom because she's white like an Almond Blossom. Actually, my grandmother is the one who picked that name. It was perfect! I loved it! Can I keep you? I will take very good care of you."

Happiness radiated from Karah's heart and soul until she sensed someone watching her every move. Managing a slow, deep breath she looked over her shoulder. Her eyes scanned the floor. It was back. The throbbing shadow that plucked her out of the van was skirting toward her across the floor. With icy fear twisting her heart she responded rapidly using the momentum of her words to gather courage.

"What are you? What are you going to do to me?" she said.

Karah took a step backward as Spot disappeared from her hand and appeared in the shadow's hand before he vanished.

"Where'd Spot go?" Karah said. "What'd you do with him? Why'd you and that HIDEOUS IT kidnap me?"

"Please calm down. My name is Isabella," Isabella's shadow said. "I'm not going to hurt you. Spot is in his favorite place. My pocket. I'm the one who rescued you by whisking you out of that van. I had no part in the plot to get you into it."

"If you can rescue people why did my family die?" Karah said. "Why didn't you come to their rescue? I want my Daddy!"

"I know you want and need your Daddy. Everyone knows that," Isabella's shadow said. "If I could I would bring your entire family back, but I don't have that kind of power."

"Then you're more proof that my prayers can't help me," Karah said.

"Oh, yes they can," Isabella's shadow said. "They already have. Think back. Last night you prayed for your life and here you are. Your prayers are heard. You just need to learn to wait and see how God answers them because He knows best. Sometimes you don't even know what you should pray for."

"What do you mean? I always know what I want," Karah said.

"Back at the rest stop you wished you were back on the road with that Dreadful Dreaddog woman," Isabella said. "Did you know she conspired to sell you to HIDEOUS IT? Would it have been good for you to get back in her car and leave with her?"

Karah shook her head.

"No, it wouldn't have. The best outcome was for God to send me to rescue you and bring you here," Isabella said. "He knew what to do because He knew what was going to take place. He knew because there is nothing He doesn't know. He also heard you hoping for a modern-day white-knight to come to your rescue. Knowing you're much, too, young to manage the wily-charms of a prince is another reason He sent me."

"I saw a woman on a horse in my brain," Karah said.

"God's way of revealing that help was on the way," Isabella said.

"If you know so much can you tell me why HIDEOUS IT wanted to buy me and why my family died?" Karah said.

"Answers to all your questions will come in due time. For now just accept that all things happen for good reasons."

"How can you even suggest there's a good reason for what happened to my family?" Karah said.

"You need to quiet yourself," Isabella's shadow said as it folded around Karah's shoulders. "I know that's a hard concept to understand, but it's true. God always turns bad into beautiful! Always! No matter what! It's also true that you're deeply loved and fiercely protected by

Him. I can tell you with absolute certainty that you have nothing to fear as long as God is the center of your life."

"How can I not be afraid?" Karah said as she wiped her nose on her sleeve. "Are you forgetting my family went up in flames? If they did, I can."

"I don't forget things," Isabella's shadow said, "and I don't just think. I know that someday you'll no longer be afraid."

"What do you know? You're 'only' a shadow," Karah said.

"I know when one door closes another one opens," Isabella said. "I know it's scary when you have to wait in what feels like dark hallways. I know God wants you to believe Jesus is your Savior - The way to His Light so His Spirit can reign inside you and He can do what I said He will do."

"How do you know any of the things you said?" Karah said.

"I know because I'm not 'only' a shadow. I'm the Angel of Well-Everything, the Chief Archangel of Khalee," Isabella's shadow said as it rose off the floor and transformed into a redheaded voluptuous woman wearing a full-length, green, silk, evening gown.

Karah was careful not to speak and spoil the magical moment. The sight of the Angel of Well-Everything stunned her. She knew from the sound of Isabella's voice to expect a woman full of passion and a zest to live life with daring style, but a DivaAngel was far beyond what she imagined.

"Why are you so quiet?" Isabella said. "Don't you believe in Angels? There are zillions of us. You just can't see us and we can't appear unless God tells us we can. We're put into action when God calls upon us to minister to His children, like you. He didn't just tell me to bring you here - He told me to personally attend to your needs."

"He did?" Karah said.

"Yes. He tells me what to do and I do it. I oversee a secret region in His Heavenly Kingdom," she said, circling Karah. "You're very privileged. Only a few humans have ever been brought here before they died and Angels are rarely seen."

"You're hot," a still stunned Karah said, rising to her feet. "You're not what I thought an Angel would look like."

"I'm told I smolder," Isabella said with a sudden accent.

"Now you're French," Karah said.

"I am the Angel of Well-Everything - Whatever I want and need to be - Whenever I want and need to be," Isabella said with deliberate charm. "The last time I appeared I dressed in rags so I could get close to a man and shock him into giving up his addiction to drugs and alcohol."

Your eyes are like swimming pools. How could he not know he was looking at a heavenly being? Karah thought.

"Yes. My eyes entice many to want to jump in and take a swim," Isabella said. "Others say my eyes hungrily eat them up."

"How did you know what I was just thinking?" Karah said. "Do you read minds? Did you hear me thinking about my grandmother? Is that the reason I suddenly smelled her perfume?"

"Yes," Isabella said.

"Is she here?" Karah said. "Are the rest of my family here? Can I see them?"

"Perhaps," Isabella said. "That's up to God."

"Can you take me to Him so I can ask?" Karah said.

"You never have to go anywhere to ask God anything." Isabella said. "He's always with you. He wants to hangout with you and be your best friend forever."

"You mean I can talk to God the way I do my friends?" Karah said.

"Absolutely," Isabella said. "He even has a sense of humor and loves to laugh, but most people don't know that about Him. They forget they're created in His image and likeness. When you get to know Him you'll know when you can't be playful. Until then, He will let you know when you cross-the-line. No one will need to wag a finger in your face."

"Did you create all of this?" Karah said, scanning her surroundings.

"Only because Jesus told me I could," Isabella said.

"Then you're like God and Jesus because you can make things happen," Karah said.

"No," Isabella said. "God only gave Angels and a few other types of beings limited powers. He created everything in the Universe. He imagined what He wanted it to be like and spoke it into existence. He devised how the sun, moon, and stars would operate; where land would rest and seas should halt; and when rain and wind could come and go. I could go on and on."

As Karah yawned a pink overstuffed chair rose out of the sand.

"Thank you," she said as she sat in it. "I'm tired and my brain is crashing from data overload. Can you imagine me without a broken heart?"

"One thing I can not do is tamper with the you-in-you. Devastated hearts are God's department," Isabella said. "He'll fix you up while growing you up. You just have to give Him all of your broken pieces to work with and involve yourself in His processes. Results don't happen overnight. You have to learn how to think your way to feeling better. Changing what you think about will change the way you feel and act.

"We're all scheduled to play in *His Unending Symphony*. We're His instruments. We each perform the parts He chooses for us. Some loud. Some soft. Some fast. Some slow. Some showy. Some plain. He's the Maestro, our Master Conductor. He will tell you when you're to get in on the action. He will also keep you sidelined in the bleachers teaching you how to tame your thoughts and tongue until you learn how to participate in harmony with others without releasing sour notes. He can't and won't put anyone on His stage that doesn't know how to ignore insults and criticism and humbly follow His instructions and love others."

"Without spells and magic?" Karah said.

"Yes. Without spells and whatnot. Now, come over here. I want to introduce you to the Angels painted on the wall," Isabella said with a flair as she shifted her weight and Karah's attention. "They want you here, too. Everyone in Khalee wants you to stay with us. Will you please give us a chance to show you how wonderful it is?"

Karah looked into the eyes of the three heavenly creatures. She already knew they wanted her there. She blamed them, even though they had loving faces, for the entrance going *whoosh* then *poof* as she tried to escape.

"What's Khalee like?" she said.

"It's a delightful community in a secret region of Heaven where combatant-type creatures and Angels live, play, and learn how to do battle against demonic forces like your friend HIDEOUS IT," Isabella said. "It's like a military base on Earth, the only difference is Camp Khalee trains Spiritual Warfare Warriors who have supernatural capabilities."

"Why does God need Spiritual Warfare Warriors when he can vanquish demons with His mind?" Karah said.

"He can and does use a swift, strong-armed approach to protect His children," Isabella said, "if that's what's best for them. But it's rare because no one grows if they don't have to fight their own battles. God gives people the opportunity to participate and employs extraordinary combat units to watch over them while they're growing up and growing stronger. More and more warriors are needed because Earth has become a horrendously evil place compared to what it used to be. Some ride in patrols on horseback from one end of the Earth to the other and through the cosmic galaxy of stars you see when you go to bed at night. You'll adore them."

Karah thought her imagination channel was going to burst. Everything sounded, too, fantastic to be true. Knowing it was time for her to decide if she was going to give the beseeching Angel of Well-Everything a chance she turned her attention to the wonderful mural of magnificent women. Her choices as she saw them: go back to Earth to live in an orphanage or stay in a breathtaking place where astonishing things magically appear and disappear. When she made what she thought was a delicious decision and vigorously nodded the flawless women stepped out of the brushstrokes used to create them. "What are their names?" she said.

"The tall one in the middle with long, white Ostrich hair is the Angel of Strength and Courage," Isabella said. "Her skullcap crown is symbolic of her great courage and leadership."

Karah studied the Angel of Strength and Courage sensing her skin had the touch of mink which caused her to wonder if the Angel standing before her carrying spears and wearing a lion's mane was also as gentle as a lamb.

"The Angel on the left is the Angel of Truth and Justice," Isabella said. "Her crown is a disk between two bullhorns. The feather that garnishes it is a scale she uses to weigh truths against lies, but she doesn't need it. She always knows who's right and who's wrong and who's lying and who's telling the truth."

While examining the Angel of Truth and Justice Karah was clearly able to see the reflection of her scales shining brightly within her eyes. She also saw a teasing smile and sensed much humor within her.

"The Angel bowing in the middle is the Angel of Love and Understanding," Isabella said. "Jewels drape from her crown and stretch across her eyes for a reason. They're a reminder for others to always see the beauty life has to offer - Beauty they will always see right in front of them if they take the time to look."

A gaze of wonderful fell over Karah as she pictured the Angel of Love and Understanding surrounded by children playing with exotic birds and wildflowers. "They have wings," she said, basking in the knowledge of their power.

"Yes. They fly like the wind whenever and wherever they want. You also need to know there are two-faced powers in the cosmos," Isabella said as the Angels became particles of paint and reappeared on the wall. "They're two-faced because they were good before they turned bad. If you let them they will talk you out of doing good things and into doing bad things. They can also cause fear to rise up in you - The kind that will cause you to self-destruct. Now, I must go," she said.

"Go?" Karah said.

"Yes. I've been summoned," Isabella said as she vanished.

"Summoned?" Karah said. "Come back! Come back! Isabella! Please come back!" she shouted as she ran searching for the heavenly being that dissolved all concern she had for herself.

"Still yourself, Karah," Isabella said from afar.

"Still myself?" Karah said.

"Yes. Calm and quiet yourself down," Isabella said. "I realize this is all very strange, but you are and will be taken care of. I don't lie and I don't break promises. No one in Heaven does."

"But I don't want to be alone," Karah said.

"You're not," Isabella said. "The Holy Ghost is here with you."

"A Holy what?" Karah said as Spot materialized in her hand. "At least she didn't take you with her. I'm never going to let you out of my sight again, not that that will do any good. Everything has a way of going *whoosh* then *poof*. There's even a ghost in here somewhere."

Chapter Three

GONNA GO BOOM!

Having selected perfect comrades for Karah, Jesus sent fresh faces marching in. Karah couldn't have been happier to see two boys her age materialize, but all she could do was gawk at them and think about how ragged and dirty she looked. A clean and barefooted Karah was suddenly standing before them wearing pink and white checkerboard pants, a pink sweater festooned with white butterflies, and thick glimmering curls draping over her shoulders.

"Are you a Warrior in Training?" the disheveled blonde boy said.

Before she could answer, Spot thought of something he forgot and zapped ruffled socks and tennis shoes onto her feet.

Karah cringed when she saw what looked like babyish socks.

Spot imagined plain socks. *Poof*, the ruffles were gone.

"I don't know," Karah said, looking herself over. "All I did was wish for a new outfit I saw in a catalogue and think the ruffles on the socks looked silly. I've never been able to do stuff like that before."

Karah's reply thrilled Spot. She was a delightful refreshing treat for him. He was happy she didn't want to let him out of her sight. He didn't want her to.

The daringly handsome boy with sculptured cheekbones and perfectly combed black, wavy hair remained silent. He was trying to recover from what her outfit changed to, not that it changed. He was all too aware of other facts that in his opinion went from bad to worse. He was told they would be escorting someone to Khalee. He didn't know it would be a girl who from all appearances and behavior was going to need more help and protecting than he'd hoped. He shrugged his shoulders, took a deep breath, and in one fell-swoop spilled their purpose.

"Excuse us for not introducing ourselves when we arrived," he said. "That's Chazz. My name is Stavvon. We came to get you. Are you ready to go?"

"What?" Karah said. "I don't want to leave. I have everything I need except a bed."

As if she'd commanded it, a pink trimmed canopy bed levitated out of the sand and slowly twirled in place as it said, "Karah where do you want me to put myself down?"

Karah excitedly led her new bed to the dragon filled with chocolate covered popcorn charms.

"Now I know why you don't want to leave," Chazz said as the dragon cracked a smile and its belly started popping. "Test your powers again. Imagine something else."

Stavvon closely observed Karah as she closed her eyes and a table with four heart-shaped stools popped out of the sand next to where he was standing. His jaw plummeted and he moved out of her new dining set's path when she told it to position itself next to her saintly statue fountain and imagined the fruit juice turning into soda pop.

"Alright," Chazz said as he filled his hands and lifted them to his mouth. "My mom won't let me drink this stuff. She says it's excessively carbonated and will cause me to go chazzerk."

"Then maybe you shouldn't swallow," Stavvon said.

"Why are you staring at me?" Karah said when soda burst out of Chazz's mouth.

"I'm wondering if you're sure you're not a Warrior in Training," Stavvon said.

"I didn't say I wasn't," Karah said. "I said I don't know. Things appear when I think of something I want. I pictured furniture I saw in a store window. *Poof* there it is. I wanted soda pop. *Whoosh* there it is."

Stavvon mused over the fine and fancy princess furniture created by what he thought was a fine and fancy prissy girl as a King's feast appeared on the table. When he saw each of their names carved in a stool he shook his head thinking, *Jesus should have sent someone to escort her to a shopping mall.*

The sight and aroma of food caused Chazz's taste buds to jump for joy. "I don't ever want to leave here either," he said as he sat down and filled his plate.

"What about you, Stavvon? Aren't you going to eat?" Karah said.

"I'm not hungry," he said. "I have stuff on my mind."

"What stuff?"

"Just stuff."

"Can't you eat with 'stuff' on your mind?"

"Yes, I can eat with 'stuff' on my mind."

"Then why aren't you eating? You looked hungry when the food appeared."

"I was and I am, but the 'stuff' on my mind is serious so I don't feel like eating."

"What's serious enough to cause you to lose your appetite?"

"Okay. You win. If you must know, I'm wondering how I'm going to get you to Khalee."

"What do you mean by 'you' getting me to Khalee?"

"It's just that you being kinda prissy, ah, could ah, could make my job a lot harder."

"You think I'm prissy? You think I'm a job? You think you're going to have to 'carry' me because I'm wearing designer pants and a sweater with butterflies on it?" she said.

"We could do that. We're Warriors in Training," Chazz said, looking up from his dinner. "See our backpacks and canteens. These letters W I T stand for Warrior in Training. We're here to rescue you."

"Do I look like I need rescuing?" Karah said, lifting her hands. "I can even conjure up made to order food and furniture. Something you two don't seem to be able to do or you would have joined in on the fun."

"You're right. We can't do that, yet. I apologize for insulting you," Stavvon said. "I didn't mean to. I would just feel better about taking you to Khalee if you looked and acted like a tomboy."

Having humored himself to the point of uncontrollable laughter because Stavvon's mind was in awhirl over Karah's flare for high fashion and home furnishings, Spot began thrashing about in Karah's pocket. Thinking he was sick when she discovered him hugging his stomach out he came between her thumb and forefinger.

"Something's wrong with my lizard," she said as a tiny pink high-back chair appeared for her to lay him in.

Ready for another dose of fun Spot thought of something else he could do. White stylish sunglasses studded with pink hearts appeared on her face.

Chazz and Stavvon secretly rolled their eyes at each other. Two things bothered them: The latest addition to her wardrobe and what she thought was a lizard. They knew it was no ordinary lizard. Experience told them that whatever Spot was might be able to take on any number of alternate forms, but neither of them wanted to reveal that possibility. They thought her much, too, skittish.

"Your lizard is cute," Chazz said as Karah took her glasses off to adjust them.

"Where'd you get it?" Stavvon said.

"Spot isn't an it, He's a he," Karah said as she put him back in her pocket.

Once again Stavvon's eyes set on Karah. He was back to wondering about her, but this time he was wondering how she would know if anything was a he or a she. When she caught him staring at her again he looked at Chazz hoping for interference.

Knowing his friend well, Chazz was happy to oblige. He quickly swallowed a mouthful of mashed potatoes and said, "So Karah, where you from?"

Chazz's question caused Karah to think about what happened to her family. Her eyes glazed over as she forced her mind to shift back to the present and said, "A place called San Diego. I'm sure you've never heard of it."

"We know where San Diego is. We were born on Earth," Chazz said. "I sprung up in Seattle. Stavvon's whole family is here. They're from Chicago."

"You're the one who doesn't know what's in the rest of the Universe," Stavvon said.

"Why do you keep looking at me and talking to me like I climbed through a rabbit hole?" she said.

"Because you're ALIVE. We had to DIE to get here," Stavvon said. "Why did God beam you up?"

"I don't know," Karah said. "I went *whoosh* and *poof*, then things started going *whoosh* and *poof*, now I'm making things go *whoosh* and *poof*."

"And so it goes," Chazz said. "When it comes to training missions we have to figure things out on our own. At least that's what Jesus, I mean Rabboni, always says."

"Are you telling me I'm on a training mission?" Karah said. "Who is Rabboni? Why did you say Jesus and change your mind?"

"We truly don't know about the mission part," Stavvon said, "or why you're here. We only know the reason must be important."

"Rabboni is our Master Teacher and the Commander in Chief of the Kingdom's Spiritual Warfare Forces," Chazz said. "The main training facility is Camp Khalee. That's where we attend boot camp."

"Boot camp?" Karah said.

"Yes. When we graduate Rabboni will give us canteen covers with symbols that represent our greatest strength," Stavvon said.

"We'll get wings, too," Chazz said.

"Aren't you a little young to be in the military?" she said.

"We're thirteen, the minimum enlistment age," Stavvon said. "How old are you?"

"Twelve," Karah said, wishing she were already thirteen.

"That must be why we're supposed to escort you to Khalee. You're still a little kid," Chazz said.

"I, too, will be thirteen in a few months," she said.

"What's a few?" Chazz said.

"Eight," Karah said.

"That's not a few?" Chazz said.

"Can we please get going? I want to get back to Khalee before I outgrow my bike," Stavvon said.

"I'm not leaving unless Isabella tells me I can," Karah said, "even if this Rabboni person did tell you to come and get me."

"Isabella? You know Isabella?" Chazz said.

"Why are you so surprised?" Karah said.

"Because Isabella doesn't involve herself with small matters," Stavvon said, "and WITs are only given missions that won't blow up in their faces until they learn how to keep things from exploding."

"I forsure feel better now," Karah said.

"Nothing and no one is going to go BOOM. Now, can we please go?" Stavvon said.

"Sit down and eat, Stavvon. You're spending the night. Karah needs to rest so you 'won't' have to carry her."

"That was Isabella," Karah said. "She's been listening to us argue."

"Cool. Now we know what her voice sounds like," Chazz said as he wiped his mouth on his sleeve.

"Didn't you hear me?" Karah said. "I said she's been listening to us argue."

"Every Angel in Khalee has heard every word we've all said or thought since we arrived," Stavvon said.

"Oh, no," Karah said.

"Get used to it," Chazz said while lifting a red pitcher with pink porcelain roses. "Trying to fight it will only wear you out."

Karah rolled a question around in her mind as she lifted her goblet so Chazz could fill it with pomegranate juice. "If you just heard Isabella's voice for the first time does that mean you've never seen her?" she said.

"Only in a picture my mom has on our fireplace mantel," Stavvon said.

Feeling privileged, Karah produced a smile and remained silent.

"I heard she's two-thousand years old," Chazz said.

"Two-thousand?" Karah said.

"Stop talking about how old I am and eat."

Spot chuckled as all hands, fingers, arms, elbows, and mouths were suddenly put in motion. He couldn't help but wonder how long it'd been since Karah had eaten as he watched her devour the roast beef, fried chicken, and mound of mashed potatoes she piled high on her plate. Knowing she wanted her escorts to have private sleeping quarters he caused her imagined solution to materialize.

"Oh, Earthling. Why do you get a bed and we only get a pup tent?" Chazz said.

"There are air mattresses inside," she said as she left the table. "It's seasonally outfitted for two boy scouts."

"Well, picture us on rubber rafts in a waterhole. It's as hot as Hades in here," Chazz said.

Once again Karah's wish was Spot's delight. Stavvon and Chazz suddenly appeared floating in a swimming pool posed in little pink boats and holding pink pineapple drinks with pink umbrella straws.

"I wasn't done eating," Chazz said, "and pink is my most unfavorite color. I also prefer coconut mango smoothies."

"Then you get nothing," she said.

Karah dove in as Chazz's boat vanished and he went under.

Needing to take care of some unfinished business, Spot swam out of her pocket as she broke the surface of the water and quickly paddled to Stavvon who was forcing himself to sip his drink without complaint. "I'm glad I finally got you alone," he said as he crept up the side of his boat. "I need to tell you something. Karah can't conjure up anything. I'm doing it. Please don't tell her. I can't remember the last time I had this much fun. She's so cute when she gets excited. Wouldn't you agree?"

"What are you? I know you're not a lizard," Stavvon said, ignoring Spot's 'cute' remark.

"You're right. My nose is, too, long," Spot said. "I'm Queen Alexia's guardian."

"Her Sacred Crocodile?" Stavvon said. "You're a sneaky little mind reader, too, aren't you? I wish I had that power."

"Trust me, knowing what everyone's thinking has disadvantages," Spot said. "It can get you into trouble. That reminds me, you need to keep an open mind about Karah. There's much more to her than meets the eyeballs."

Suddenly anxious for more sparring Stavvon climbed out of the pool looking like a teenage poster boy modeling dry hair and clothes. Karah examined him wondering why he wasn't wet. In that moment, she was also suddenly dry and wrinkle free with restyled curls.

"I see you didn't change your mind about us sleeping in a pup tent," Stavvon said. "Is it filled with a bunch of pink puppies?"

Chazz dove inside and was disappointed to find no puppies, pink or not, when Karah discovered a charming nightgown on her bed. Stavvon quickly joined him. They hid their eyes and closed their tent flaps when they saw her put it on over her clothes.

A dazzling full-length mirror framed with twinkling lights materialized as she admired the fit and snapped the elastic bound ruffles on her wrists. Her squeals brought Stavvon and Chazz back to their knees. The sight of her admiring herself in front of a mirror caused Stavvon to snicker and whisper in Chazz's ear. Holding in his laughter, Chazz listened intently as Stavvon filled him in on his chat with Spot. They then stopped laughing and changed their attitudes when they saw her kick her shoes off, jerk her socks loose, and toss them like they do. "Maybe she isn't completely prissy through and through," Stavvon said as they withdrew their craning necks.

When she crawled into bed Karah found a children's bedtime prayer plaque on the pillow, just like the one her grandmother had given her. Her eyes transformed into beams of light. She gently picked it up and made a dent in her pillow to put Spot in. As she nuzzled up next to him and kissed his pinhead nose her mouth stretched into a wide yawn. "Goodnight, Isabella," she said with the prayer clutched against her chest.

"What about me?" God said in her mind.

"Who said that?" she wondered.

"You should already know," He said. "Before you go to sleep, I want to tell you something else you should know. Stavvon is in charge. I put him in charge because he's the top Warrior in Training in Khalee and Jesus personally selected him to be your lead escort. When he asks you questions please don't argue with him. You are a 'job' to him because his mission is to get you safely to Khalee. He questions everything so he can succeed at his missions."

Astonished and ashamed, Karah scolded herself for forgetting to say goodnight to God and for suspecting Stavvon was purposefully being macho and trying to sound smarter because he was a boy. *"Of course he would be. He's no longer just a boy,"* she reminded herself. *"He's a Warrior in Training and will soon have wings and perhaps be able to walk out of paintings like the Angels. They both will."*

Now ready to sleep, trapped and captured Karah rolled over knowing she wouldn't dream that night because she was already living a real-life fantasy. She wearily but happily closed her eyes as one of Spot's eyes popped open so he could keep watch while sleeping.

Chapter Four

ROUTE B TO KHALEE

Spot PATIENTLY WAITED for Karah to wake up and discover bunny slippers floating over her head. When she did, he wasn't disappointed. She sprouted a rapturous smile and shoved her feet into them, just as he knew she would. She also skipped to the table, sat down in front of a breakfast buffet, and right on cue said, "Time to get up WITs. I created toad and grasshopper pop-tarts for you. I'm sorry for reacting to all of your questions and getting upset about the way you kept looking at me yesterday. I'm sure you had your reasons."

Stavvon didn't groan when he crawled out of his tent and saw her sitting at the table swinging a foot with a pink bunny slipper on it. He reminded himself she's supposed to be 'more than just all that' and smiled at Spot.

Chazz wrinkled his face as he pulled his stool out from under the table and watched her force a forkful of eggs into her mouth with what was left of the bacon.

"It no longer matters that the bacon is all gone," Stavvon said. "Rabboni told me it's time for us to get moving."

"When?" Karah said.

"Just now," he said.

"Just now? How?" she said. "I didn't hear anyone."

"Telepathically," he said, pointing to his head.

"In your head?" she said. "Just like that? He told you we have to leave?"

"Yes, just like that," Stavvon said. "I thought I heard you say you weren't going to argue with us anymore."

In that moment, a pink backpack appeared in Karah's hand. "I didn't imagine this," she said, staring at it.

"I did," God said from afar.

"Sounds like the Power-To-Be is on our side now. You better go get your things," Stavvon said, "which don't include the jeweled bracelet you're wearing. Put it back where you found it. Technically, it belongs to God like everything else," he said.

Chazz kept his mouth shut. He didn't want to get in on this exchange. He was more interested in the toad and grasshopper pop-tarts. He hurriedly stuffed them into his backpack thinking they might be needed to appease a slithering serpent during a hasty escape.

Spot rode Karah's shoulder like a parrot as she returned to her mirror to imagine what she wanted to wear. Moments later with a right hand salute she marched up to Stavvon and Chazz sporting pigtails, blue jeans, a pink sweatshirt, and a pink baseball cap that made her almond shaped eyes pop like saucers of fudge. The bracelet she'd left on her bed popped back onto her wrist simultaneously.

"One tomboy reporting for duty Sir, with a bracelet I'm guessing is mine to keep," she said.

"That's a tomboy?" Chazz said.

"A spoiled tomboy," Stavvon said. "She gets everything she wants. What's with that?"

Chazz slowly shook his head as he left the table to stand next to Stavvon in front of the mural of the Angels.

"What are you waiting for?" Karah said.

"The Gatekeepers," Chazz said.

In that instant, the group portrait of Angels vanished and the archway reappeared.

Karah gasped when spangles of sunshine beamed in showing off a vast ocean of wildflowers under a dawdling sun. She dashed through bees serenading unopened buds heading for a pink bicycle parked between two shiny silver and black ones. "I saw this bike in a Christmas catalogue a long, time ago," she said, "but I didn't just think-it-up. I only remembered it when I saw it."

"That's probably why there's a gift card in the basket," Chazz said.

"I just upgraded my impression of you to spoiled-rotten tomboy," Stavvon said as she picked up the envelope.

"I wonder who it's from," she said.

"We'd like to know too," Chazz said. "Read it outloud."

Karah did.

Dearest Karah:

This bicycle is a gift from Us. Please accept it as an apology for the fun someone has been having with you at your expense. He meant well. He just didn't look at the big picture and realize you thinking you have special powers would be detrimental to your safety. We also want to thank you for putting the bracelet back where you found it. Because you didn't take it, We can give it to you.

Our Eternal Love,

God the Father, the Son, and the Holy Ghost

"Wow!" Chazz said. "That's unheard of. Don't let anything happen to that card. The last time God penned something with His own hand was the Ten Commandments."

After examining the card and the envelope Karah held it out to Stavvon and saw what she thought was a couple of scheming, mischievous WITs. "It was you guys," she said. "You were reading my mind and making stuff appear and disappear so you could play tricks on me. Weren't you?"

"It was Spot," Stavvon said. "We don't have the power to read minds, yet."

"That's right. We only have beginner powers," Chazz said.

Karah pulled Spot from her pocket. When he covered his eyes as if that would hide him she knew he was the culprit. Even so, Chazz's limited power advisory was a sore reminder that they couldn't protect her by causing serious harm to come to something or someone if need be. She put the card from God in her back pocket while asking Him to protect her.

The tassels on her bike's handlebars started blowing and its wheels started churning when she put her feet on the pedals. Stavvon and Chazz confirmed that her bike knew where it was going by letting it take the lead and following close behind.

Karah was happy to be cycling through the meadow on her new bike, but she didn't like being in the lead. She was secretly worried about what there was to keep her safe from and wishing she was following Stavvon and Chazz so she wouldn't be on the frontline if an attack occurred.

Spot was riding high with his head poking out of her shirt pocket, but he didn't have to stand to see out. He created it with transparent material. He was thrilled to see a cluster of magnificent green and yellow butterflies fluttering toward them knowing their presence would shift Karah's mind from the gloom and doom she expected to encounter. As usual, his prediction was unerring. Karah released her grip on the handlebars and touched their lively wings as they gracefully caressed her with little kisses. When they perched on her arms and legs the majestic strum of an enchanting harp announced the arrival of a white translucent butterfly studded with diamonds set in drops of 24-karat gold.

"Isabella is here," Stavvon said.

"That's not Isabella," Karah said. "I thought you said your mother has a picture of her."

"She does, in her butterfly form," he said.

"You're also a Divine butterfly?" Karah said.

"I am the Angel of Well-Everything," Isabella said as she landed on the tip of Karah's nose.

Karah closed one of her eyes to keep both of them from crossing as Isabella cocked her head and wings and gave her a hearty look of approval.

"Hello Isabella," Stavvon and Chazz said in singsong unison.

And they thought I was prissy, Karah mused.

"That's right. I heard you boys judging Karah by her appearance. That wasn't nice," Isabella said.

"Karah," Chazz said, "don't forget to watch what you're thinking."

Feeling like every fantasy character she'd ever read about Karah laughed herself silly as her mind filled with happiness. She was Alice. She was Dorothy. She was an imagined Harriet Potter on a thrilling magic carpet ride without the carpet. She then looked to the sky and her joy was abruptly extinguished by the sight of a monstrous pair of hands forming a donut hole in a snarling black cloud rushing toward them. Electrifying fear spiked through her like an uncontrollable fever when HIDEOUS IT poked her head through wearing a venomous smile and dove out like a dive-bomber.

Three bikes, two heavenly boys, and one terrified tourist were suddenly racing through fearsome thunder, angry lighting, pounding rain, and golf ball-sized hail as gut wrenching laughter bellowed from HIDEOUS IT's underbelly. Karah didn't care that painful welts were appearing on her arms and legs. She didn't care that wet gobs of hair were plastered over her face. She also didn't care that she couldn't breathe or see where she was going. She was just glad to be on a bicycle that could go very, very, fast and relieved to have WITs closing in on both sides of her pulling swords out of their handlebars so they could shield her from harm.

"Don't be afraid, Karah," Isabella said as she appeared as a ghostly apparition. "Progy will get you out of here."

"That's Progy?" Chazz said as he menacingly swung his sword at HIDEOUS IT.

"Who's Progy?" Karah said as HIDEOUS IT knocked her baseball cap off her head.

"Me," her bike honked.

"My bike?" Karah said.

"We're close to an escape route," Stavvon said.

"Just get me someplace safe where ghouls can't pop out of the sky," Karah said.

In that moment, Progy swerved and Stavvon thrust his sword out and down on HIDEOUS IT's fiendish fingers as she snagged one of Karah's pigtails. Stavvon and Chazz gave each other disturbing looks when her left pigtail hit the ground next to a bloody, blue finger. They knew of few places in the cosmos where satanic forms couldn't reach through something or someone to snatch her.

When Progy came to a very, unexpected sliding halt Karah pushed gobs of hair out of her eyes and saw all three bikes perched on the edge of a river without a bridge to the other side. "I thought Progy knew where he was going," she said.

"I do," Progy honked as Stavvon thrust his sword at HIDEOUS IT.

"That's Route B to Khalee," Chazz said as he struggled to get his sword out of HIDEOUS IT's grip. "There's a ferryboat in a tunnel on the bottom of the river."

"How do we get to it?" Karah said.

"We dive," Stavvon said as he aimed his sword at the rushing water.

"I'm not diving in there," she said as lightning cracked over her head and Stavvon took another stab at HIDEOUS IT.

"Do you want to live?" Chazz said as HIDEOUS IT's bleeding hand reached for her remaining pigtail.

Without warning all three bikes dove into the river. Karah didn't have time to catch a mouthful of air. She swallowed a mouthful of water.

Bubbling, gurgling screams didn't stop coming out of her until she was far under and discovered she didn't need air to breathe.

Having the time of his life, Stavvon smiled radiantly with his hair floating overhead.

"This is the bomb," Chazz burbled with his feet pitched like boat oars.

Karah gawked at them while the crystal tunnel's magnetic force drew their bikes toward the bottom of the river. The slightest touch of Stavvon's sword sliced an opening in the side. Once safely on the deck of what looked like an elongated peapod with fancy curly cues on each end their passageway closed on its own like an open wound. Karah looked up and around trying to deal with the whirlpool of bewilderment swirling inside her head. A quick glance told her there was room for nearly twenty passengers. She also noted the ferry had everything most boats have other than a room with a toilet and realized she hadn't needed one since her foiled capture at the rest stop potty-house.

There was no doubt in her mind that unheard of Angels and beings in the Heavenlies saved her from the grotesque being that wanted to rip her off her bike with hopes of tossing her into, yet, another Universe. She sat wondering how many players were on Isabella's miraculous team when she appeared fluttering against the Ferry Captain's cheek as he skillfully maneuvered his ferry at full-speed with a tiny rudder poking out the stern.

When visitors gathered outside the crystal tunnel and swam alongside the ferry as they waved to her Karah didn't know if she'd ever get used to expecting the unexpected. She only knew she didn't want to get used to seeing exotic gold and silver fish-creatures riding sidesaddle on the backs of magnificent great white lions. She was enchanted by their floating gowns and swaying ponytails, thinking their pointed chins and beaded earrings very fashionable.

"Those are the RiverAngels," Stavvon said. "You're now in the Great Divide."

When her visitors bowed and swimmingly rode out of sight she turned to Stavvon and Chazz wishing she'd come out of the river dry the way they did and said, "Now I understand why you thought I wasn't prepared for this journey. I wasn't. I'm still not."

Spot designed another look for her. Fashionable white shorts, a pink shirt, and lip gloss were part of this instant makeover. He even replaced the pigtail cut off during the fight for her life.

"Thank you Spot," Karah said, "but I think I am going to need all the protective gear I can get. Please reimagine me in jeans and hiking shoes."

Spot did as she asked.

Karah's continued efforts to adjust to their world caused pangs of respect to prick Stavvon and Chazz's hearts.

To compensate her for all she'd been through the ferry was suddenly sailing through a glorious layer of hot pink roses, courtesy of Jesus.

Spot looked at Stavvon and mouthed, "I didn't do that," as Karah reached over the side to pick one.

Chazz was fast on his feet. He jumped up and positioned himself to grab onto her in case she toppled over the side like a ship's anchor.

Seizing the moment to take a much needed break Stavvon leaned back in his seat reasoning through the complexities surrounding his KarahMission. He wanted to know why escorting her turned into a death-defying assignment and why Isabella, God's Senior Archangel, was seemingly babysitting her or possibly all of them.

Chapter Five

POISON MOUTHED DIT

THE REALIZATION THAT their journey to Khalee was going to take longer than she hoped became clear to Karah when she rode off the ferry and came bouncing out of a cave and into a forest alongside Stavvon and Chazz. She'd pictured her ship sailing into a glamorous dock where she and her escorts would disembark. She'd even envisioned the sights and sounds of throngs of people cheering their arrival. Not so. Karah had never been in the wilderness so this surprise outcome was not her idea of a good time, but it was wildly exciting for Stavvon and Chazz who were hooting and hollering as if they'd entered an amusement park with thrill rides. Impressed by how easily they could ride their bikes over large surface tree roots, as if simply chasing geese out of a garden, she decided to give it a try and refrain from complaining.

Stavvon's initial assessment of Karah was spot-on. She wasn't someone anyone could picture lapping up the great outdoors and she was often called prissy, but only by well meaning people. Moreover, she was painstakingly gentle, kind, and loving. She didn't just have a good heart - She had a great heart and cared about people to a fault. She also loved art and music. She especially cared about music. Her father was also creative and artistic. She wanted to succeed in her music and become a pianist, but she had no desire to be famous. She was just passionate about everything and threw herself into whatever she enjoyed doing with vigor and determination.

While contemplating her dismay about winding up in the wilderness Karah learned her first important lesson: Don't daydream in a world you know nothing about. She was unaware of a flock of deadly birds whizzing toward her with dangling foot-long, bloodsucking legs until Stavvon said, "Duck," and Progy darted toward a cave.

"What are those things?" she said.

"They're called BatFish or BatBirds depending on whether they're swimming or flying after you," Stavvon said.

"This cave is a Godsend. They're surprisingly afraid of the dark," Chazz said as he rode to safety behind them. "They won't come in here."

"You don't want to tango with them. Not ever. They're covered with deadly goo," Stavvon said. "If they'd touched you, well, never mind they didn't."

"You're as white as a marshmallow," Chazz said as Karah climbed off Progy and stretched her legs.

"I'm going to stay that way if this keeps up," she said. "I'm glad I asked Spot to redress me in jeans."

Amazed she could make a half-hearted joke about her most recent close encounter, Stavvon and Chazz started laughing. Karah also laughed. She couldn't believe she did, but she knew it was because she felt safe with Stavvon who paid close attention to everything going on around him and everyone else. She was extremely grateful for that. She also appreciated Chazz's comic relief. His welcomed expressions smoothed the fierce edges of the strange and frightening Khaleean countryside.

All were happily taking a break from their cold and bumpy bike ride until a cloud of orange smoke appeared at the opposite end of the cave. The air lacked the energy to move when an ominous blonde on a bicycle t-whopped out with the tactics of a beast and rode toward them with a twisted cantankerous face.

"Please tell me I'm in the throes of a nightmare," Chazz said.

"Now you're as white as a marshmallow. What's wrong?" Karah said. "She's just a girl."

"That's no girl," Chazz said. "That's Gigo. Our mission just took an ugly turn."

"It hadn't already?" Karah said.

"Believe it or not, things did just get worse. Gigo is Khalee's poison mouthed antagonist with retractable fangs," he said.

"Keep your voice down," Stavvon said. "If she hears you none of us will be safe from the predatory gleam in her eyes."

"Don't get in a stare down with her," Chazz said as he stepped in front of Karah like a shield. "She's a DIT. A Demoness in Training."

Karah gasped.

"Not really," he said. "She just acts like one. Make sure you don't look into her black holes of gravity."

"Her what?" Karah said.

"Her eyeballs," Stavvon said. "Don't get in a stare down with her."

"What's going on? Why am I here?" Gigo said as she dropped her bike.

"Believe me, we didn't request your presence," Chazz said.

"Who's the pipsqueak?" she said.

With a look of indigestion Gigo began sending Karah disdainful currents proving Stavvon and Chazz hadn't exaggerated her eye power.

Chazz nudged Karah to the side of the cave and broke the connection with a glare of his own aimed at Gigo.

"I hope you have a spare set of eyeballs. Your's are spinning in place," Stavvon said. "We told you not to get in a stare down with her."

"You think I wanted to," Karah said. "Her eyes are like magnets. They grabbed mine."

Gigo studied Stavvon and Karah with an idling growl until she realized what Karah was.

"How'd a human get here?" she said.

"You have to ask?" Chazz said.

"Forget the how. I know the how," Gigo said. "I want to know what she's doing here."

"She has a name. It's Karah," Chazz said.

"I want to know what you're doing with an Earthling," she said.

As Gigo sidestepped Chazz to get next to Stavvon, Karah dished her smugness back and said, "Isabella asked the boys to escort me to her house."

Greatly surprised by Karah's sudden grit and that Gigo's eyes were no longer having the intended affect on her, Stavvon and Chazz stood speechless.

Gigo was also caught off guard. She turned on Karah and tossed her head and said, "The boys? How cozy! I don't believe you. What would Isabella want with the likes of you?"

"Come with us and see for yourself," Stavvon said.

Karah shuddered like a pinball machine as Stavvon's invitation ricocheted through her body.

"I'm in," Gigo said. "Hanging out with a little Earthling should be good for a stupendous if not stupidious time."

"Karah stay away from Gigo as much as possible," Stavvon said as he walked her to Progy.

"Stay away from her?" she said. "How can I do that when you asked her to ride to Khalee with us? Why'd you do that?"

"Rabboni just told me to," Stavvon said.

"Why?" she said.

"We already told you we're never told why we're supposed to do anything or how," he said.

"Even in Heaven there's a *Need To Know Policy*. You'll see for yourself when you get to Khalee. Think of Gigo as your Caiaphas," Chazz said.

"My Caiaphas?" Karah said. "What's a Caiaphas?"

"A Caiaphas isn't a what. Caiaphas was a who. Hellooooo. New Testament Caiaphas. The High Priest who led the conspiracy to crucify Jesus. If Jesus had to have a Caiaphas who are you to complain when you're given one?"

"What are you talking about?" Gigo said. "Are you planning a Prissy Princess Party or are we going to Khalee?"

"Karah are you ready?" Stavvon said.

"Yeah, Karraaah. Are you readddyyy?" Gigo said.

"You first, Gigo," Stavvon said.

"She's not going to be able to keep up with me," Gigo said.

"Don't worry. Karah will be right behind you," Chazz said.

"Ooooh, but shouldn't she go first?" Gigo said. "After all, she is a little Earthling."

"Okay, Karah you lead," Stavvon said.

Feeling like a pawn in a game of chess Karah pleaded mentally with Stavvon and Chazz for a way out. She pulled Spot from her pocket for an added sense of security.

"Where'd you get that?" Gigo said.

"What? My lizard?" Karah said.

"That's not a lizard. Its mouth is, too, long," Gigo said.

"No it isn't," Karah said as she climbed on Progy.

Progy had heard enough. He didn't want to listen to another debate about whether Spot was or wasn't a lizard or about who was going first. He gave Karah the escape she wanted by racing off like a thoroughbred bolting out of a starting gate.

"And they're off," Chazz said with a vigorous salute.

"Wait for us at Creator Creek," Stavvon said.

Seeing Gigo's jaw plummet caused Karah to smile. She was happy Progy left her in a cloud of dust, but nervous about being separated from Stavvon and Chazz. She quickly began looking out for whatever she might need to be on the lookout for. She tried to remain vigilant, but was easily distracted by what she considered to be more than her fair-share of wondrous sights.

Her eyes danced with the sun as it flickered through tree branches where she spotted squirly creatures flying like wilderness rockets. While they followed her path and lifted her spirits delightful purple polkadotted ponies with shiny red hooves and gold metallic eyes as big as cue balls raced to catch up with her. Her heart was overcome with joy when blue bellied eagles soared across her path to welcome her and join their wilderness friends.

Karah became so used to the unexpected she wasn't even a tad surprised when an albino girl wearing a turquoise cape skipped out from behind a bush and handed her a bouquet of giggling flowers as she turned into a llama so she too could run with the ponies alongside her. When they all arrived at Creator Creek her wilderness friends leapt, skipped, galloped or soared off as Progy performed his usual sliding spin stop and honked his horn telling her to get off.

Unable to contain her excitement, Karah ran into the sweet smelling stream with her fistful of flowers and shoes on and climbed up the side of an enormous boulder with water gushing around it. She didn't mind when she slipped and splash-landed in the creek. She burst out laughing. The trees laughed too, but not because her precious flowers were floating and giggling their way downstream. They laughed because Karah was laughing and having the time of her life.

"Be careful," a rainbow trout said as she cupped her hands and thirstily stuck them in the water.

Karah's joy instantly vaporized. She froze and let her drink of water slowly trickle through her fingers and back into the stream when she saw what looked like a snake working its way toward her. When she clearly identified the something as a snake she noisily thrashed out of the water.

The slimy-lime-green reptile rose straight up and glared at her with swirling fluorescent eyes that were in a-huff and a-twitter about something. "What'sss wronggg withh youuu? Whyyy areee youu lookinggg att meee likeee thattt? Don'ttt youuu knowww thatt III ammm aaa sacreddd creatureee?"

Karah didn't answer the snake hissing and bobbing in the shallows of the creek in front of her. A snake was a snake, sacred or not, especially one with wings for ears that wiggled back and forth like little fans. Her head bobbed, but she wasn't saying yes. She was following the snake's dancing beat.

"I'mmm Aamirrr. I'veee beennn waitinggg forr youuu. Whattt tookkk youuu sooo longgg tooo gettt hereee?"

Karah mustered up some courage and crept toward the twitty, twirling snake. "Why were you waiting for me?" she said.

"III wuzzz tolddd tooo beee hereee. Dooo youu thinkkk III woulddd haveee gottennn innn thisss creakeee ifff III hadn'tttt beennn ordereddd tooo? Nowww, takeee meee outtt offf theee waterrr. You'reee supposeddd tooo takeee meee tooo Isabella'sss houseee withhh youuu."

"*Eeeesch,*" Karah thought. She didn't want to go near Aamir let alone pick him up and take him to Isabella's.

"III saiddd I'mmm aaa sacreddd creaturrrr. Didn'ttt youuu hearrr meee? You'rrrr supposseddd tooo takeee meee outtt offf theee waterrr. Innn theee nameee offf Jesusss, III commanddd youuu."

Karah still couldn't do it. "I can't touch you," she said. "You're a snake."

"III beggg yourrr pardonnn. I'mmm aaa Sacreddd Cobraaa. Neverrr minddd. III wasss justtt tolddd tooo gettt outtt byy myselfff."

"Who told you, you could do that?" Karah said.

"Whooo dooo youuu thinkkk?"

Karah was stupefied when Aamir propelled himself out of the water and turned into a stick in midair as he came flying toward her, and equally dumbfounded when she unwittingly reached out and caught him.

"Attt leasttt youuu knowww howww tooo catchhh."

"III knowww howww tooo hearrrr, tooo, sooo stoppp hissyyy-yellinggg attt meee," she said.

"Welll, justtt listennn tooo youuu."

Chapter Six

CANDY-EYED CROC

WHILE KEEPING A vigilant eye on her Aamir-stick and waiting for Stavvon and Chazz to arrive Karah prayed that the one filled with all-the-charm-of-a-shark wouldn't be in the picture when they did. Even so, she wasn't surprised when Gigo rode into sight alongside them. Her hands curled into fists as she watched Gigo dismount and advance toward Progy so she could knock him over in poltergeist fashion while strutting pass him.

Karah wasn't the only one who witnessed Gigo's antics.

Aamir was trembling and hissing, "Lettt meee attt herrr. Lettt meee attt herrr."

Prog was begging, "Please. Oh please, Ms. Karah. Please let Aamir go get her. She did that on purpose because I ditched her. I got sand in my tassels when she knocked me over."

The idea of turning Aamir loose on Gigo sounded more than

perfectly swell, but Karah's whispered and restrained response was, "Be quiet, both of you. I can't hear over your whining and hissing."

Spot raised his snout over the edge of her pocket and gave Aamir and Progy 'stop it' stares.

Karah didn't notice. She'd tuned in to Gigo in time to hear her say, "I want to go hunting with you Stavvon. Karah can stay here with Chazz and play with her stupid, stick toy." Nausea climbed her chest as she watched her hustle after him when he entered the forest. *"I hope you get lost and never come back,"* she mused.

"Don't think like that. Don't let Gigo get to you," God said in her **mind. "You're going to have to learn to love and accept her - Warts and all."**

"Her?" Karah thought. *"Never!"*

"What's going on in your clickety clackety brain?" Chazz said.

"I heard a voice in my head. I think it was God," she said.

"What did the voice say?" he said.

"That I shouldn't let Gigo get to me," she said.

"That was God," he said.

"He also spoke to me last night. Does this mean I can now send and receive messages?" she said.

"You'll never be able to communicate like heavenly beings until you die," he said, "but you do have the ability to receive God's messages. You don't have to worry about sending Him any. He knows your thoughts before you do. There's no escaping that hard fact. The upside is, He can keep you from saying or doing whatever stupid thing you're about to say or do."

"If I'm not a heavenly spirit why would He want to speak to me?" Karah said.

"He doesn't only speak to us," Chazz said. "He talks to people trying to steer them straight, but He rarely speaks directly. He usually employs His Spirit to guide through suggestive thoughts. If you haven't sensed that before you either weren't paying attention or you thought you were coming up with your own ideas. The reason I know it was God that chimed in your mind is because the other voices would have urged you to punch Gigo in the face."

"What other voices?" Karah said.

"A Christian's old nature and Satan have powerful internal voices," Chazz said. "You can always tell who's prompting you. If what you sense is moral, uplifting, encouraging, and gives you peace it's coming from God. If it's immoral, condemning, discouraging and causes confusion it's your old nature or Satan.

"God only speaks truth. Satan only tells lies. When God says you're loved believe it. When the other voices say you're unloveable turn a deaf ear to them. When God tells you to ask your mother for permission, ask her. When the other voices tell you to do what you want because your parents will never find out, don't do what you're thinking about doing. Life can feel like a game of ping-pong between God and Satan with you as the ball in play. The good news is you get to decide who wins. It's called Freewill. I'd hitch my wagon to God if I were you and always do whatever He says even if it does sound like a suggestion. He tells you what you should do, but gives you a choice by not making you. If you don't do what God suggests at some point in time He will let you suffer the consequences."

"Why would He do that?" Karah said.

"So you can learn from your mistakes," Chazz said. "It's your choice, not His. God doesn't force Himself on anyone."

Karah hung on Chazz's every word greatly surprised that he carried serious knowledge tucked inside his joke-tossing demeanor. He was more scholarly than he looked or let on which meant he was smart and humble. She now knew why a jokester like him was a top Warrior in Training alongside Stavvon.

"My parents didn't listen to God and got a divorce," Chazz said. "Satan kept putting ugly thoughts in their heads so they would complain and argue. Over and over God told them to stop, but they didn't and gave up trying to be happy. Here's something else that's scary."

"There's more?" Karah thought.

"Satan can also answer your prayers," Chazz said.

"No way," she said.

"Yes way," he said. "It's a safe bet that someday you'll ask God to bring the man of your dreams to your doorstep. Satan will know because he watches and listens. When the time is right God will answer your prayer. In the meanwhile, Satan will deliver what looks and walks and talks and acts like God's answer. You'll thank God not knowing 'Mr. Right' is the Devil in disguise and go kaboom! No fragments found!"

"How can I make sure I don't fall for an evil-baited answer? How will I know the difference?" she said.

"Ask God before you get involved with anything and then pray, listen, and watch for His answer. If you truly want one, no matter what, you'll get one. The problem with most people is they don't think they need His help. They take matters into their own hands. When they do they unwittingly invite Satan to mess their lives up."

"Has Satan messed Gigo up?" Karah said.

"We're not supposed to wonder about other people. Jesus says we're supposed to mind our own backyards."

"Where's Stavvon? What's taking him so long?" she said.

"Are you worried? Do you think God would let something happen to Him?"

"No," she said as her face softened.

"He won't let anything happen to you, either. You need to learn to control your thoughts. Now chillax and stop fretting. Stavvon can deal with Gigo, if that's what's worrying you. If it's your stomach that's making you edgy, I can assure you Stavvon will bring back something to cook for dinner by the time I'm done building a fire," he said as he grabbed a sharp rock and began using it to dig a hole.

"Chazz," Karah said as she helped him dig, "Isabella *whooshes* here and *poofs* there. She even makes sounds when she does. Why didn't she zap me directly to Khalee?"

"I don't know," he said, "but there's always a good reason for everything the Angels do."

"Why does everyone have to figure everything out on their own?" she said.

"So they will grow from participating in the process. Stavvon can figure most everything out that's why he's Batman and I'm his Robin."

"And I'm a prisspot?" she said, laughing.

"We don't think that anymore. Now, we think you're primitive."

"Primitive?" she said.

"Only compared to us. Now, I'd better finish building a fire in the pit instead of getting you fired up. I don't want Stavvon to come back and find out you've got more steam in you than you showed yesterday."

"I said I was sorry," Karah said. "I was just-"

"What?" he said.

"Nothing. Nevermind," she said.

"Come on, spill. You can't start saying something and stop," he said.

As she thought of her family Karah filled with heartache and leaned into a tree unable to speak. Sensing she was deeply distressed Chazz was glad instructions had been given to spoil her rotten for a while. He stopped prodding her and lit his erector set of logs that created a blazing inferno campfire and caused a truce with nearby termites. "Where's your lizard with the long mouth? I'm hungry," he said with a teasing wink.

Gigo quietly and slowly approached with a purposeful expression as she secretly watched Karah and Chazz warm their hands over the fire. She then quickened her pace and her mouth began flapping, but not in its usual snide way. "I saw Isabella," she said, pointing. "She's fluttering around in the bushes at the foot of that hill."

Karah took off anxious to tell Isabella how ghastly Gigo was behaving. Before she was out of earshot she heard Gigo say, "What a sissy. I knew she'd go running off to look for some dimwitted butterfly." She then heard Chazz say, "Karah's no sissy. No girl has ever collected more wood for a fire than I have and she didn't swat at bugs making nests in her clothes the way I did. I've never seen you get your hands dirty other than making trouble for others. And woe to you for thinking Isabella didn't hear you call her dimwitted. That's not one of the 'D' words used to describe her."

She looked over her shoulder at Chazz, her hero, while carefully picking her way through a briar patch and stumbled upon a lion basking in the sun, "You're no butterfly," she said.

"I'm not a real lion, either," the lion said.

The lion arose and stood on its hind legs with its paws on Karah's shoulders as Stavvon stepped into their midst with his hands full of trout. His pupils popped as he watched the lion transform into the Angel of Strength and Courage.

"Okay, Stavvon. Now you've seen me alive and up close," the Angel of Strength and Courage said. "When we're finished here you can go back to Camp Khalee and tell everyone until then close your mouth. I have something to tell you. Gigo didn't see Isabella fly into this brush area like she told Karah. She saw a lion, me, take cover in here. She's about to get a taste of what she hoped Karah would encounter."

When the Angel of Strength and Courage changed back into her lion form and charged off in pursuit of her prey Stavvon and Karah sprinted after her. Chazz sensed the lion was heading for Gigo and was not at all surprised when it knocked her down and pinned her to the ground with its jaw.

"Apologize to Karah for telling her you saw Isabella fly into those bushes when it was really me, a lion," the Angel of Strength and Courage said through tightly clenched teeth.

Gigo's terror stricken face pleaded for help as her stubbornness kept her from complying.

An outraged Aamir turned into his slimy-lime-green, lava-eyed self and spit his forked tongue out at her nose as he slithered up to her neck, "Biteee downnn harderrr," he hissed.

"Okay. Okay. I apologize," Gigo said.

"Nowww thattt youuu knowww I'mmm nottt aaa STUPIDDD STICKKK TOYYY youuu won'ttt playyy withhh Karah'sss lifeee againnn willl youuu?" he said.

Once again, Gigo refused to answer.

"Answer Aamir or I will bite down harder," the Angel of Strength and Courage said.

"Okay! Okay! I promise not to make any more trouble for Karah," Gigo said.

"My report is going to read that your time in exile didn't teach you anything," the Angel of Strength and Courage said as she strutted triumphantly out of camp on four beautiful paws.

Gigo gathered her shattered nerves as Aamir stared her down with his swirling lava-lamp eyes. He then shimmied his way to Karah, snaked up her leg, put his head in her hand, and turned back into a stick.

"I can't wait to tell everyone I saw the Angel of Strength and Courage," Stavvon said.

"That was her?" Gigo said.

Stavvon turned to Karah with a knowing smile and began funneling the newly disclosed information through his mind. The fact that Gigo had been exiled explained why she hadn't been seen for a long time. It was also now clear to him why Jesus brought her back and tossed her into their midst. "Karah, did you know your stick is Moses' sacred staff that God turns into a Sacred Cobra anytime He wants or needs to?" he said.

"Yes, I know about Aamir," she said.

"Is there anyone or anything else you can tell us about?" Chazz said.

"Well, I did meet the Angel of Strength and Courage once before and also the Angel of Truth and Justice and the Angel of Love and Understanding," she said. "Isabella introduced them to me. She also gave me Spot. Sometimes his jewels glow like Christmas lights."

Karah stared at Stavvon hoping all the mysterious Angels and beings she'd encountered only wanted her to have an exotic vacation. Stavvon stared back knowing most of the Kingpins in the Kingdom had formed a heavenly posse that undoubtedly consisted of countless others. While carving sticks into fish roasting spears he unfolded more facts that created an unmistakable chain of logic that pointed to only one reason why the key citizens of Khalee would go into a tailspin over her. He watched her back as she headed for the lake to wash her hands and tried to picture her as what she was supposed to become.

"Stavvon, are your eyes glued on Karah for a reason?" Gigo said.

As Gigo turned her attention to the pile of candy between her thighs and dug through it with savage selfishness, Karah turned her attention to Stavvon. She liked the way he handled himself and how he always remained relaxed and in control. She saw him as someone who would pluck the moon and stars out of the sky for a worthy person. *"On

Earth you would be called a Knight in Shining Armor. Maybe God changed His mind about giving me the saving prince I prayed for," she mused.

She continued watching him perform chef-tricks without a kitchen as she sat on a stump in front of the fire listening to Chazz's frightening stories about ogres feeding on teenagers who sleep next to lakes in the forest. She didn't want to miss one of his moves. She was especially impressed when he pulled oranges out of his backpack and spliced them around the middle with his thumbnail so he could work the peels off in two halves. She was equally amazed when he smashed berries in them and filled them with water. In awe, she readily accepted the refreshing orange peel cup of raspberry juice he handed her.

Spot wasn't missing anyone's moves. His glowing jewels were filming Karah's entire journey for safe keeping in Queen Alexia's Heavenly Hall of Records and Archives.

Progy wasn't missing anyone's moves, either. He was involved in nearly every one. Like Spot and Aamir he adored Karah and wanted to stay close by her side. He felt blessed to be included in the exceptional assembly of friends relaxing and cooking dinner over a campfire fire until they realized it had been, too, quiet for, too, long.

"Where's Gigo?" Chazz said.

In that moment, distant screams eerily echoed through the forest.

They jumped to their feet.

"That was her," Stavvon said.

Karah was scared. The heart wrenching sounds filled her with dread. She became even more concerned when Stavvon pulled a log out of the firewood pile knowing he intended to journey into the unknown to look for her. She didn't see an antenna on the back of Gigo's head that would give off a tracking signal.

"I'm going with you," Chazz said as he wiped his hands on his pants.

"Not this time," Stavvon said. "One of us must stay with Karah. If I'm not back in thirty-minutes take Route C to Khalee and get her out of here."

"Route C," Karah said. "What's that an explosive cannonball ride?"

"You're not far off, but don't worry," Chazz said. "Stavvon can find anything in the dark."

After watching Stavvon march out of site Karah turned her attention to Chazz. She didn't believe he wasn't concerned because the boy who joked about everything had nothing light-hearted to say about his fellow WIT going off alone into the black of night when evil is out in full-force.

Wanting Stavvon to have a beacon of light to follow back to their campsite she put log after log on the fire to keep it blazing. She also wanted it crackling and sparkling so it could help vanquish whatever came barreling into their campground.

"You've made the fire large enough for us to get a glimpse of a gang of grizzlies coming at us from the other side of the mountain," Chazz said.

"It's something I can do. At least we'll be able to watch them rip us to shreds," she said.

"You're starting to sound like me," he said.

Karah gave Chazz an appreciative smile. She knew the fire wouldn't even thwart a baby dragon, but it made her feel better. Having encountered evil beings during the day and adding a wannabe DIT to the mix was more than she thought she should have to bear.

"Chazz, I wish the fire was a crystal ball," she said as she forced her eyes open. "Maybe it would tell us why Jesus told Stavvon to take Gigo with us."

"I would second that if fate telling paraphernalia weren't forbidden," he said.

"Why is she allowed to be soooo?"

"Nasty?" Chazz said.

"Yes, that!" Karah said as a yawn forced its way out.

"I wish I knew," he said, looking to the stars.

Karah shifted her attention to the stars as well and was reminded of God's presence. She gave up her diehard plan to stay awake so she would hear the slightest sound of Stavvon or anything else creeping about in the night. Chazz covered her with a blanket he pulled out of his backpack. He, too, was cold and tired but he wasn't going to sleep during his KarahWatch. It was a good thing he didn't nod off because Jesus had arrived at their encampment in His Eagle form and would have known. He was also keeping an eye on Karah from deep inside a leafy tree while contemplating the affects His two WITs and one possible DIT were having on her.

Stavvon returned to camp with Gigo pacing him from behind looking sluggishly defeated and much less dangerously certain of herself. Karah awoke when brittle sticks snapped beneath their feet. She lifted her head and took one long, look at Gigo's mottled face thinking, "*She clearly escaped a great tussle with something,*" and laid her head down with a grimacing look. Chazz also got an eyeful when he looked at Stavvon's log-club. He could tell it had been used on something. He surprisingly didn't say a word while he rolled his sleeping bag out next to the fire and climbed into it.

Aamir curled up close to Karah when Gigo began ripping wrappers off her chocolate bars and started chomping, smacking, and slurping on them. There was one long period of silence after another shattered by tearing, chomping, smacking and slurping. No less disturbing than glass bottles rolling down a sloped paved alley in the middle of the night. Even the green-eyed, orange-winged, noisy-night crickets were annoyed, but they could crawl away and they did. In a hurry!

"Karahhh," Aamir said. "I can't sleep. I promiseee youuu. Ifff III hearrr oneee moreee wrapperrr tearrr I'mmm goinggg tooo coilll myselfff aroundd herrr anddd I'mmm nottt goinggg tooo askkk forrr permissionnn."

"You're going to have to beat me to her," Karah said. "I'm ready to flip out, too."

When Gigo cut through the night with a sloooower than ever rip, Karah was true to her word. She lept to her feet, but she didn't get to 'Gooo gett herrr' as Aamir hoped. Gigo jumped up screaming at the same time when she saw and felt a crocodile's jaw inside her candy bag. Stavvon quickly responded by calmly grabbing a rock and throwing it at the ground next to the croc's head.

The angry crocodile, complete with a candy wrapper clinched

tightly in its iron jaw, cut loose thrashing and whipping through camp like a punctured high pressure steam hose.

"I hope that wasn't Shazak," Stavvon said as he reflected on his decision.

"The way I see it," Chazz said, "you did her a favor. I heard she's allergic to chocolate."

Chapter Seven

POWER OF THE FLAME

THE FINAL LEG of Karah's wilderness training didn't look like a long one, but it was. Only birds in flight could see how far the distance spanned. Every time they entered a clearing she saw more mountains between her and the large one they were headed for. Worn out and weary, she took on Gigo's role as Miss Irritable. Taking notice, Progy rocketed across the meadowland with Aamir curled up in his basket and Karah pressing on her pocket so Spot wouldn't bounce out. When darkness fell he turned his two handlebar nighteyes on and the one inserted in the back of his seat so he could see friends or foes coming from any direction. He was carrying precious cargo. Nothing was going to get Karah, not on his watch.

When they arrived at Isabella's all three of Progy's travel-by-night lights burned out simultaneously and wouldn't turn back on no matter how hard he shook himself. Spot crept out of Karah's pocket and winked at her to prevent her from being able to hear what he was about to say. She tugged on her ears as he leapt into the basket and perched on Aamir and said, "Progy, Isabella is red-faced. She just told me to tell Karah to get off of you and that you're to go into town and take Aamir with you."

"Did she burst my bulbs?" Progy said. "Is she upset because I took off with Karah without permission?"

"Youuu haveee tooo askkk," Aamir said. "III justtt hopeee sheee doesn'ttt thinkkk III haddd anythinggg tooo dooo withhh yourrr warttt braineddd impetuousnesss. Ifff III didn'ttt wanttt aaa rideee tooo townnn I'ddd punctureee yourrr tiresss withhh myyy tongueee."

"I didn't hear you hissing at me to stop," Progy said. "You were enjoying the ride as much as I was and you know it."

"You'reee righttt. III wasss anddd Isabellaaa knowsss," Aamir wailed in one fangfull.

"Snap out of it," Spot said. "Even I didn't get exiled for playing tricks on Karah. Your roles on her Protective Services Detail aren't going to end anytime soon. Now, get going. Isabella is waiting for you at Spike's."

"What are you going to do?" Progy said.

"Get some rest," Spot said. "I need to recuperate from having spent the past four days recording Karah's every thought and reaction. Why else would I be talking instead of transmitting Isabella's orders."

"III hopeee youuu didn'ttt senddd Queennn Alexiaaa thattt shottt offf meee pickinggg myyy youuu knowww," Aamir said.

"What? Your teeth?" Spot said. "Why would you care about that?"

"I'mmm nottt asss snaketifieddd whennn myyy fangsss areee showinggg," he said.

"If you don't stop thinking like that you're going to get turned into an Angel's purse, shoes, and a belt," Progy said.

"Attt leasttt I'lll stilll beee gorgeousss," Aamir said.

"Get over yourself and get going," Spot said.

Karah's ears unplugged as Spot leapt for a grassy knoll and turned his jewel lights off. She quickly dismounted and searched for him until Progy began pedaling away. "You can't leave, too," she said.

Aamir, the only one who could wave, set his little ear wings flapping.

Karah only had one thing to turn to - A brightly glowing candle visible in the window of a house otherwise hidden in darkness.

Remembering Stavvon and Chazz telling her there's always a reason why Angels do whatever it is they do only gave her a fleeting moment of comfort. She felt dangerously unprotected and sensed a force moving in on her. As someone or something blew in her left ear she no longer cared if she might stumble on something. Her feet started moving to get next to the candle. She felt her way toward the house and fell hard on some steps where she discovered a handrail to use as a guide to work her way up to and along the porch.

The candle's flame burst 6-inches high and froze in a bright piercing shade of yellow when she arrived at the window. A moment later it turned vibrant red and then shimmering green like an automatic yield-stop-go traffic light. *"Is someone switching its channels?"* her thoughts poured out over the pounding of her heart.

Once again she drew on what she knew: Progy, Spot, and Aamir would never leave her somewhere she wasn't safe. Nevertheless, she wanted to stay near the candle and not go off looking for a front or back door in the dark.

She knocked on the windowpane. No one answered. She smushed her face on the glass and saw a bed with the covers pulled back and a crumpled pillow that looked as if someone's head had just been there. She knocked again, but harder. Still no response. She cupped her hand around her ear and leaned against the glass listening for a television or radio playing in the background. Nothing. *"Would anyone in Khalee even have a radio or television?"* she wondered.

Struck by another possibility, she tried to open the window so she could take the candle. *"It's not like I'm going to steal it,"* she told herself. *"I'm only going to use it to find a door with a doorbell."*

Tiny buzzing balls of glass filled with twinkling lights rushed toward her and formed a massive sphere that took off as she struggled with the window. She ran after it following a path that led to an amazing garden where four sculptured bushes were surrounded and illuminated by flaming torches.

"There's fruit inside the leaves," the sphere of twinkling balls said.

"Inside the leaves?" Karah said.

She picked a shiny red one to see if it was true. Sure enough it tasted like a luscious apple. Her next pick was a yellow leaf with brown spots. It was what she thought it would be, a ripe banana. She plucked a purple leaf and bit into the sweetest plum she'd ever tasted. A red watermelon leaf with black seeds was her next delight. When she spotted bright yellow leaves she quickly passed over what she thought were sourly sights.

"Hello Karah. Welcome to the *Fruit Garden of the Heavenlies*. My name is Corissa," a young woman said as she magically appeared. "You can eat the lemon leaves. They're sweet. Try one. See for yourself. All the fruit in the Garden of the Heavenlies is always perfectly ripe and sweet."

Karah was no longer interested in the fruit leaves. Her eyes were examining the canteen strapped to Corissa's hip that was covered in lion skin and trimmed with a ring of bronze fur.

"I'm Nony," another young woman said as she appeared wearing an amusing smile and a canteen attached to her belt that had miniature eyeballs and question marks on it.

"And I'm Jasmine," a third young woman said when she too appeared with a canteen.

Karah studied Jasmine's black velvet canteen cover adorned with sparkling jewels and gold beads and looked again at Corissa's and Nony's knowing they were full-fledged Warrior Angels because there were tiny wings on their covers which meant they could fly like the wind wherever and whenever they want.

"I'm sorry for staring," she said. "I was wishing I had a canteen with a special cover like all of your's."

"Well, we wish we had a crocodile in our pocket," Nony said. "Did Spot enjoy his ride?"

"He's not a crocodile. He's a lizard," Karah said.

"Are you sure?" Corissa said. "He has an awfully long nose."

"Why does everyone keep saying that? Hey. How'd you know I named him Spot?" she said.

"Word travels fast in Khalee," Jasmine said. "We also heard you met Gigo."

"She's pathetic," Karah said.

"Oh, no! Look out! Your nose! Your eyes! Your ears!" Nony said.

"What?" Karah said.

"You're transforming into Gigo," Jasmine said.

Karah quickly felt her face and discovered nothing was happening. "That wasn't nice," she said. "I thought you were serious. You really scared me."

"Did you think it was nice to make fun of Gigo?" Corissa said.

"I just sounded like her didn't I?" Karah said.

All three Warrior Angels nodded.

"Thank you for telling me," she said. "I don't want to start talking and acting like that miserable DIT. Oops. I shouldn't have said that, either. Huh?"

Pleased with Karah's quick catch Nony gave her an appreciative look and said, "Did you enjoy the fruit?"

"Yes," Karah said.

"Each one of those bushes represents one of God's prominent creations. They're symbolic," Jasmine said.

"Like the designs on your canteen covers?" Karah said. "What do your's symbolize?"

"We can't tell you," Corissa said in mysterious fashion, "but we can tell you what the fruit bushes represent."

"The ever blooming heart-shaped bush represents God's never ending love for His children," Nony said.

"The sun-shaped bush gets double pleasure sprouting up in this garden," Jasmine said. "It gets to watch the sun rise like a kite on a string and travel East to West bringing daylight to everyone in the world."

"The star-shaped bush represents one of God's favorite creations," Corissa said. "Stars do more than decorate the sky. They supernaturally contribute to astrological energies in outer space in ways that only He knows."

"There's a very, special StarAngel named Bettina," Nony said. "She arranges the stars."

"She has a big night ahead of her because Queen Alexia requested a star show in honor of your arrival," Jasmine said.

"Will they burst across the sky?" Karah said.

"Yes, but people on Earth that are too busy to wonder about the majesty of it all will miss them," Nony said.

"Children take the time," Jasmine said.

"God allows Bettina to entertain them by creating connect the stars pictures," Stavvon said as he unexpectedly rushed up behind them.

"He loves hearing little children say, 'I see a cuddly bear,'" Chazz said as he materialized alongside him.

"Why didn't you tell me you could *zap* yourselves around?" Karah said as she stood to greet them.

"We can't yet. We go *whoosh* and *poof* just like you do when there's a need," Stavvon said.

"Do you think Bettina would *zap* me up in the sky with her sometime so I can watch her arrange the stars?" Karah said with great anticipation.

"If I see her I'll ask," Corissa said.

"If you see her?" Chazz said, swirling his eyes. "There's no such thing as 'if' when it comes to seeing Bettina. You can't miss her. She wears a black skintight bodysuit studded with stars and she has the body for it."

"She can wear outfits like that," Nony said as she pulled on her muffin-top tummy, "and she's a gorgeous blonde."

"Stavvon, did you come to take me the rest of the way to Isabella's?" Karah said.

"Look no further," Nony said.

Laughter filled the air when Karah looked over her shoulder at the house and saw the candle in the window expand again as if to say, 'Hi, remember me?'

"I had the feeling she was in there," Karah said, "but why is she in the house when she could be out here with us?"

"She has her own way of doing things," Stavvon said while also wondering what Isabella was up to.

"She's always busy because she's God's senior ranking Archangel,"

Nony said, seeing Karah's disappointment. "She might not even be inside."

"She has to be," Karah said, "unless she can be in two places at once. Look at the candle."

"You mean one of Isabella's eyeballs," Chazz said.

"Yes. I guess," she said as she turned to Chazz and back to the candle. "See. Look. The flame is getting taller again. Why's it doing that? What's she doing?"

"She's using it to squeeze your brain until your eyes pop out. See how tense you are," Chazz said.

"Stop it, Chazz," Corissa said. "Can't you see this is all somewhat frightening for Karah?"

"She knows I'm teasing. Don't you Karah?" he said.

"Karah," Jasmine said, shaking her head at Chazz, "Isabella is only examining you. She needs to know everything about you so she'll know how to best guide you as your life begins to change."

"And change it will," came another daring detail from Chazz.

"Chazz if you don't bridle your tongue I'm going to zip your lips," Corissa said.

Karah saw the look in Corissa's eyes and knew she meant every word.

So did Chazz.

"Jasmine is right," Nony said. "You have no reason to be concerned about Isabella getting inside your head. You're going to adore her as much as everyone in Khalee. She's nothing short of fabulous."

"And 'D' for Dazzling," Jasmine said.

"I heard she throws the most exotic parties imaginable," Stavvon said.

"Just don't get fooled into thinking she's a pushover. There are two other 'D' words used to describe Isabella. Dramatic and Demanding," Chazz said before he could stop himself.

Corissa kept her promise.

Chazz's lips were immediately zipped.

Karah tried not to laugh when she saw a lock dangling from one corner of his mouth instead of a pull tab.

"The good news is she only cuts demons to pieces with her laser-sharp mind," he managed to mumble.

Corrissa caved in and burst with laughter when everyone else did.

"Gotta love me!" Chazz mumbled.

"Only because God commands it," Nony said, smiling.

"Did we tell you Isabella loves music?" Jasmine said.

"I play the piano," Karah said.

"I've heard you," Corissa said.

"When?" Karah said.

"At your school talent show two-years ago. I was the one who caused that horrid girl to have to go to the bathroom so she'd leave and stop trying to cause you to make mistakes."

"You did?" Karah said. "I always wondered why Jules got up and ran off. I was only glad she did."

"The plans of foes are always foiled sooner or later. We all heard you say you wished she wasn't there and that's not all," Jasmine said.

"We heard your teachers say you're a walking, talking, living, breathing, angel," Corissa said.

Karah had no idea. Her heart soared upon hearing such wonderful words used to describe her as she set her sights on the moon-shaped bush. "Is there an Angel who gets to supervise the moon's comings and goings?" she said.

"My dad said if an Angel could hang the moon it would be Isabella and that all the MaleAngels would fight for the right to hold her ladder steady," Chazz mumbled.

"Chazz!" Corissa said.

"My dad is the one who said it. I only mumbled it," he mumbled in defense.

Karah knew Chazz's lips weren't going to be flapping anytime soon when the lock vanished.

"She's also the 'D' for Daring Protector of The Earth Portal, this garden," Stavvon said.

"I heard she eats the fruit of the Heavenlies to maintain her figure," Chazz mumbled.

Nony jumped up as Jasmine's jaw hit the ground and grabbed Chazz to haul him off before Corissa could get her hands on him.

"Earth Portal?" Karah said.

"Jesus ascended directly into this garden after He was crucified," Corissa said. "You're sitting in the same spot."

"For real?" Karah said, jumping up.

"Yes, and these non-fruit-bearing bushes sprouted leaves with fruit inside when He did," Jasmine said. "That's why it's called *The Earth Portal* and *The Fruit Garden of the Heavenlies*. Believers also rise up right here because they're Jesus' fruits."

"God's aphorism: 'I AM yesterday! I AM today! I AM tomorrow!' is inscribed on the back of each leaf," Stavvon said.

Karah fingers fumbled over the tangerine leaf in her hand as she found the words and read them.

"Someday you will rise up right here, too," Corissa said.

"Yeah, when you return from the Underworld," Stavvon said.

"Underworld?" Karah said.

"I hear Bettina," Jasmine said as Corissa groaned and Stavvon filled with remorse for speaking out of turn about a very, serious truth.

Karah turned quiet when everyone else did, but she wasn't led astray. She knew Stavvon said something he wasn't supposed to and planned to interrogate him later.

Chazz brought her mood back when Nony released him from his time-out and Corissa unzipped his lips so he could eat a fruit leaf she handpicked for him. She hoped it wasn't a cure for the words that usually pop out of his mouth. She didn't want him changed. She enjoyed his personality very, very much just the way it was.

She reached for Corissa's hand as Corissa reached for Nony's and Nony reached for Jasmine's - Thinking they were all fabulous reflections of the Dazzling, Daring, Dramatic, and Demanding D words.

Linked with a new family she gasped with great awe as a brilliant trail of stars raced across the sky and formed a giant fireball that burst into an array of sparkles on the silhouette of distant mountains. When the last flicker melted on the horizon she slowly tipped to the left until her head gently came to rest on the ground.

Everyone was right. Isabella did have her own way of doing things and everything always went according to her perfect plan. She materialized standing over Karah and caused Corissa, Nony, Jasmine, Stavvon, and Chazz to vanish simultaneously. She lingered for a long while never before having felt the presence of a child with the depth of Karah's inquisitive passion and sweet kid-like frankness.

Her mind filled with possibilities as she left her sleeping in the garden and reappeared in bed with her head in the pillow that earlier looked as if someone had just been there. She then summoned her diary that appeared fanning its gold pages until the flame in her left eye erupted right where she wanted to engrave Karah's spirited image.

Chapter Eight

SAFE HOUSE

AT THE FIRST hint of morning light, Karah consumed the sight of Isabella's polished rock house nestled amidst purple blossoming vines dangling from ancient sycamore trees. The tree vines she loved, the tree trunks not so much. She backed away from the wood casts of fused distorted bodies with anguished faces thinking, *"Maybe they're supposed to scare crows away from the fruit leaves."* She then turned to wondering why she'd been left sleeping outside all night.

"So you'd wake up in My garden with Me," God said from afar. **"Those tree trunks are My Scarecrows. They're vivid reminders that those who follow Satan are condemned for eternity."**

"No wonder I wanted to get away from them," she said.

When God went silent Karah climbed the steps of Isabella's porch and found an outdoor living area with black and white floor tiles, an ornate red wicker couch stuffed with hand painted silk cushions, a round dining table with four chairs, a porch swing, and an antique desk loaded with books in a corner next to an overstuffed chair by a Tiffany floor lamp. A star-shaped window with gold butterflies embedded in the glass drew her to peek inside the house.

Thinking Isabella was asleep she decided to sit outside and wait where she had a panoramic view of the lush mountains she'd just trekked through. When she spied a silver box of stationery next to a sprawling white flowering plant she couldn't resist the temptation to examine the unusual letter opener on top of it. A ghastly nerve shattering alarm went off as she picked it up. Expecting Isabella to come charging out of the house to scold her she quickly put it down and flung herself into the porch swing. The scent of something foul rushed past her, but no one charged onto the scene of an incident that set off a siren that could clearly be heard throughout Khalee. She filled with relief when it stopped ring-ring-ringing in her ear. She felt lucky as opposed to what happened in a museum when she touched something she wasn't supposed to touch. She still didn't think she was responsible for the nail falling out of the wall and the priceless painting smashing to the floor, even though everyone told her it wouldn't have if she hadn't touched it.

"I'm never-ever-again going to touch anything that doesn't belong to me. I'm not even going near that stationery box," she told herself. Karah did, however, have exciting thoughts of coaxing Chazz into touching it the next time he came over. She chuckled while imagining his reaction until a bristling breeze stirred up glistening windchimes. After finding them with her eyes she lifted Spot so he could see them up close. As if they recognized him and wanted to say 'Hello' the dangling charms began chiming a familiar melodic tune that caused her to waltz with him pressed against her chest. They twirled and swirled until the breeze withdrew and the chimes became still.

Growing weary she curled up in a chair and put Spot in her lap. From there he leapt onto Isabella's desk and turned on his jewels. He was refreshed and his spirits were high because Karah was finally where everyone wanted her to be. Forgetting her promise to herself, Karah picked up Isabella's eyeglasses and put them on.

"I thought you were never-ever-again going to touch anything that doesn't belong to you," God said.

"Do you watch my every move and hear my every thought?" Karah said as Spot enthusiastically nodded.

"100 percent of the time," God said.

"You're all a bunch of spies," Karah said, smiling. "I can't get away with anything."

In that moment, a pair of arms reached over her shoulders and covered her with a patchwork quilt. Through Isabella's wire rim glasses Karah gazed into Isabella's calculating eyes that didn't have a trace of pride.

"Good morning. Did you sleep well?" Isabella said with lingering smoothness in, yet, another accent as she lifted her glasses off Karah's nose.

"Now you're Italian," Karah said.

"I am whatever I want and need to be whenever I want and need to be," Isabella said as she crossed her legs and exposed red leather, kneehigh, laceup, boots with spiked heels. "How about you? Ever want to be something you're not?"

Karah nodded.

"Tell me. Tell me, now. What do you want to be that you're not already?"

"Someone's sister and daughter," Karah said.

"Done."

"Does that mean you're my mother now?" Karah said.

"You now have so many mother-types and sister-types you're not going to be able to count them."

"Did you say that because you know I'm lousy at math?" Karah said.

"You're not lousy at math. You just don't apply yourself. You prefer creative endeavors. I only know you'll never make it as a scientist because you'd never dissect a frog, something Progy is very happy about."

"Progy? Why would he care about that?" Karah said.

"Because he's not a bike. He became one for you. He's a frog, the Prince of Guardian Creatures. You already know Aamir is a Sacred

Cobra. Now it's time for you to meet one of your other traveling companions," Isabella said as Spot jumped into her arms.

"Can I keep the name Spot?" Spot said.

"My lizard can talk?" Karah said.

"Because he isn't a lizard," Isabella said as she put Spot on the floor. "He's Queen Alexia's Guardian Crocodile."

Karah gasped as Spot transformed into his usual 7-foot size before her eyes. "He is a crocodile. A huge one," she said. "I'm so embarrassed. I was so sure he was a lizard I wouldn't listen to anyone."

"Let that be a lesson, but your mistake was an easy one to make. Not everyone knows how long a croc's nose is supposed to be, especially when they're reduced to little, lizard-size. He and other guardian creatures are sacred. They're everywhere in Khalee."

"Everywhere?" Karah said.

"Yes, be careful to never hurt one. Crocs, frogs, snakes, hmmmm, let's see, oh yes, other sacred animals you need to be warned about are cats, hippos, hawks, eagles, lions, dogs, and beetles."

"Crocodiles," Karah said as a thought struck her. "One came into our lake camp. Stavvon hit it with a rock."

"I saw what happened," Isabella said. "Stavvon didn't hit Shazak. He didn't intend to. He purposefully threw the rock at the ground next to her jaw. He only wanted to scare her away."

"Shazak. That croc has a name?" Karah said.

"Yes, and Stavvon was right to do what he did. He couldn't take any chances with you present. There are demonic beings in the cosmos that can take on the shapes and forms of good beings. Stavvon was tricked once. He won't let it happen again. Corissa, Nony, and Jasmine, went with him to help explain the candy-eyed croc in camp incident to the Majestic Beings Court Council. Shazak filed a complaint against him."

"Chazz said that his dad said that all the MaleAngels wish God would let you climb a ladder and hang the moon," Karah said with an enormous smile.

"That sounds like something Chazz and his father would say," Isabella said.

"You like him, too, don't you?" Karah said.

"Yes, very much. He's a delight and Stavvon is a little Prince. Now come, walk with me," she said. "I have something to show you. Be on the lookout for beetles. They're easy to miss. You don't ever want to step on one."

"What would happen if I did?" Karah said.

"You'd be fed to Shazak."

"What?" Karah said.

"I'm teasing," Isabella said. "Nothing will happen that I can't put a stop to if God lets me. Everyone around here is fanatic about sacred animals, even waterholes and prayer ponds. Don't go near the wrong ones."

"Is your letter opener sacred? When I touched it a five-alarm siren went off," Karah said.

"You didn't just touch it. The alarm went off because you picked it up. I would have come charging out of the house as you imagined if you hadn't promptly put it down."

"I thought it was a plain'ole letter opener," Karah said.

"Not hardly. If I open something with that it will light on fire. I meant to put it away before you got here. I forgot. I, too, have been distracted by your arrival. Now let's get you cleaned up and head into the village before I get lynched for hoarding you."

"Who would want to lynch you?" Karah said.

"Nearly everyone in Khalee. They're all waiting to meet you. Yesterday Helki, our head hippopotamus, came over twice to see if you'd arrived. She wasn't the only one. I had to remind everyone I had my own plans. Those plans have nearly transpired so we shouldn't dally. They know you're here. They heard Corissa, Nony, and Jasmine, discussing you last night."

"Why were they discussing me?" Karah said.

"They were flipping a coin to see whose bedroom you were going to share."

"No one has to share a room with me," Karah said. "I can sleep on the couch."

"That wasn't the point of the toss. They were trying to win you."

"They all wanted me? Who won?" Karah said.

"Like always, I did. That's where we're going. I'm taking you to your bedroom."

Karah was completely baffled when Isabella headed toward the blossoming sycamore trees. "If you're going to show me my bedroom shouldn't we be going into the house?" she said.

"Does your bedroom have to be in a house?" Isabella said.

"Isn't that where they usually are?" Karah said.

"You're in Khalee. We do things differently. Look over there under those vines. I created it while you were dancing with Spot."

Karah ran to a little bedroom cottage built with the same polished rock used to construct Isabella's house. It had identical pink stained glass windows and yellow shutters. It also had a *Karah's Cottage* sign above the door. She'd never moved as fast as she did while trying to get inside. She was so excited she tried to get through the door before lifting the latch. When she bounced off the door she didn't yell ouch, the door did. She tried again and went in laughing. Her laughter quickly quieted down when she saw her cottage furnished with the furniture conjured up for her in the mausoleum she was beamed into from Earth. In addition to her bed, table, chairs, and pedestal mirror, there was a short-legged closet chest between two windows, a desk with an oil lamp, and bookshelves filled with age-old books. Upon seeing the same author's name embossed in gold letters on each book it was clear to Karah that she was going to be learning a few things from Rabboni, Khalee's Master Teacher. She removed a book from the shelf anxious to discover what He had to say about anything until Spot strutted in and climbed up on her bed. She followed his tail as it pushed a door open and saw a little room with a sparkling pink porcelain drinking fountain. She then noticed her closet door handles were frogs with rings in their noses. "Are those Progy?" she said.

"Not hardly, just replicas," Isabella said. "Do you think he would let someone pierce his nose? His depiction is also carved in your bedposts. He's in town right now with Aamir. They met friends for dinner last night after a tête-à-tête with me. You'll see them later today."

"Can everyone in Khalee hear what I say and change into whatever form they want?" Karah said.

"Only a few can hear everything. Most can only take on one form or another. Progy being the Prince of Guardians can take on the form of any being or object he wants. He could be me right now, but he wouldn't dare. Now look in your closet. Hurry up," Isabella said.

Karah did. She opened the doors, stared inside, looked at Isabella with a blank expression, and closed them wondering what she was supposed to have seen.

Isabella opened the closet herself when Karah didn't react as expected and found it unacceptably empty. "Tootsie! Where is the Karahwardrobe I ordered?" she said as she closed the doors.

There was sudden banging and clanging coming from inside the closet. When Isabella and Karah each opened one of the two doors they found a terribly embarrassed little woman inside with pins in her mouth, ribbons draped around her neck, a tape measure in her hand, and clothes flung over both her arms. "I'm so sorry I'm late," the seamstress said as she kicked over a pile of hangers. "Isabella, please forgive me. Please. You must be Karah. Please forgive me, Karah," she said.

Karah tried to climb into the closet with the seamstress when she saw togas like the ones Egyptian Queens wear in movies. There was an especially beautiful white one trimmed in pink and adorned with gold leaves. It even had matching gold sandals with pink and white straps. "Isabella, can I please put it on?" she said.

Without delay Isabella agreed.

"Our little Karah looks grown up now," Spot said as he watched Isabella show her how to tie the straps.

"Whoa. What have you been eating? You need some breath mints," Karah said. "I can smell your big throat from over here."

"Someone has been hanging around Chazz, too, much," Spot said as he playfully knocked her over with one easy swipe of his tail.

Isabella absorbed every morsel of the interchange and smiled as Karah got up thanking the now not so nervous seamstress who was climbing back into her closet to leave. "Yes, Chazz has already had an affect on her. Stavvon has made his mark as well," she said while Karah compared their reflections in her mirror.

Karah loved her new toga, but she was still wishing she could dress like Isabella in exotic garb that looked like it came from a far away never-ever-land.

"When you're me you can wear whatever you want, wherever you want, whenever you want," Isabella said with a daring gleam in her eyes.

"I keep forgetting you can read my mind," Karah said.

Startled by the sudden sound of a drill Karah spun around to see where the noise was coming from. No drill was in sight, but sawdust was swirling out of something being carved in the molding at the top of her mirror frame. A woman sitting on a throne was exposed when lingering sawdust blew out of the design.

"Who's that?" Karah said.

"Queen Alexia. Oh, no. I can't believe I told you," Isabella said.

"Isabella, how could you?" Queen Alexia said as she jumped to her feet and vanished.

"I'm in trouble now," Isabella said.

"Where'd she go?" Karah said.

"Don't worry. She'll be back," Isabella said. "But no matter what, you can't tell anyone her image is carved in your mirror frame. Don't let that tasty-fact pop out of your mouth the way it just did mine."

"Why can't anyone know?" Karah said.

"Because she doesn't want anyone to know what she looks like," Isabella said. "She needs to walk among Angels and beings anonymously. She can't if everyone knows who she is."

"I thought you did everything for her?" Karah said.

"Rabboni told me your mind works like an electronic data-sorter," Isabella said. "There are some things Queen Alexia likes to take care of herself."

"I've never even met Rabboni," Karah said. "How would He know if my mind is a, what you just said?"

In that instant, one of Rabboni's books burst open and a 'Rabboni Knows Everything About Everyone and Everything,' banner flew out and pasted itself to the wall above her desk.

"Did He do that?" Karah said.

"To remind you to never question Him," Isabella said.

"Why is He listening to us?" Karah said. "Why would He care about what I think or say?"

"Stop asking questions," Isabella said. "I need to finish telling you why no one can know Queen Alexia's image is carved in your mirror so we can go. If you tell someone they'll believe you and come here wanting to see her; when they do she'll disappear."

"Why are you worried about that happening?" Karah said.

"Because the citizens will think you lied. You don't want anyone thinking you've lied about anything. Make sure you don't. An Angel named Ezer will be listening to see if you do. We'll know you didn't, but we also don't want anyone to know Queen Alexia is involved in keeping an eye on you."

"If you need to keep an eye on me why do I have my own cottage?" Karah said. "Why aren't I going to stay inside your house with you?"

"You're not here so we can control you. You're here to learn how to control yourself," Isabella said. "You need to become independent. You'll not be treated like a child, not in Khalee. Your training and trials will occur as needed."

"Training and trials," Karah said. "I thought it was going to be wonderful living here. Now I have training and trials to worry about on top of being afraid of getting in the way of animals, touching anything when I don't know what it is, evil beings taking on the shapes and forms of good beings, and someone thinking I'm lying when I'm not."

"How is that different from Earth?" Spot said.

"No one gets sent to the Underworld for telling LWLs," Karah said.

"What's an LWL?" Spot said.

"A little white lie," Karah said.

"A lie is a lie. There's no difference between black, gray, and white, or big, medium, and small. When was the last time you told an LWL?" Isabella said.

"When I was at the dentist," Karah said. "He asked me if he was hurting me. He was. I told him he wasn't because I didn't want him to feel bad."

"There was a reason he asked you," Isabella said. "You must learn to be truthful no matter what."

"You mean I should have told Gigo she's a DIT?" Karah said.

"No, that's not what I meant," Isabella said. "Don't tell people things that will make them want to rip your head off. Just be honest about everything with compassion. There's always a way. Now let's get going."

Fast on Isabella's heels Karah tossed her backpack on her bed and rushed out the door behind her.

Chapter Nine

GUARDIAN PASSAGES

KARAH'S LEGS WEREN'T the only things tiring out as she tried to keep up with Isabella's fast pace. Her mind was drained from contemplating the unknowns she knew Isabella was keeping from her. She wanted to know why Isabella became jittery when asked certain questions. She was baffled by all the ghastly do's and don'ts that sounded like an endless list of things she should have written on flashcards so she could memorize them. Rabboni's supernatural interest also confused her. Nevertheless, the key cause of her angst was now a hill covered with tree creatures that had eight fat tentacles for branches. Equally menacing were blue streams of light coming from their bloodsucker knobs creating powerful eerie rays on the ground.

"Come on, Karah," Isabella said. "Hurry up."

"I don't want to walk through those. They're creepy. Spit is coming out of their knobs. Ouch," she said, pointing, "that one pinched me."

"You hurt the Octoghouls' feelings. You shouldn't have called them creepy, but they shouldn't have responded by pinching you," Spot said. "I'll go have a talk with them."

Karah watched with amazement as Spot crocked up to the Octoghoul that pinched her. She was nervous for him. He was only one crocodile against many tentacles. Things did get testy, but Spot only had to snap his jaw at one tentacle to get all the Octoghouls to turn stiff and close their knobby suckers.

"They're necessary," he said as he returned to her. "They secure the entrance to and from Khalee's Spiritual Warfare Headquarters. Get ready for more strange fun. The base's second string defense, the Hedgemaze, is straight ahead."

"Make sure to stay behind me. We have to enter in single file," Isabella said.

"I don't see an entrance," Karah said.

As she spoke a section of the bushes trembled and ripped apart creating an opening.

"I'm not going to ask if I made that happen. I know I didn't," she said as leaves vigorously lifted at her feet.

"Then you'd be wrong," Isabella said. "I gave you the power to open and close this Hedgemaze when you come and go."

"I have powers now?" Karah said.

"A power. One power," Isabella said, "and only because the Hedgemaze was told to respond to your voice. Now, will you please get inside?"

Karah raced into the deceitful web of passages as a wolf or something cried out, quite certain something bad was about to happen. It did. Dozens of long, hurried tongues popped out stealing licks of her arms, legs, and face. Grabbing onto Isabella's full skirt she held it up in front of her face like a shield.

"They're only tasting you to see if you're really you," Spot said. "They're required to make sure someone or something didn't impersonate your voice."

"How would they know what I taste like? Nevermind, I don't want to know," she said as Isabella turned and gave her a look.

Karah forced herself to recover by focusing on the wonderful things she was told about the inner village and that it was filled with fun and lively inhabitants because there was going to be a party. She was also set at ease by a sudden refreshing hint of moisture in the air. A big change from the scorching heat she encountered during her journey. Nevertheless, her mood fizzled out again when the waist-high Hedgemaze instantly grew twice as tall bringing sudden darkness upon them.

"Spot, please come up in front of me and turn your jewels on. I can't see anything," she said as she separated her feet to create a path for him to croc through.

"Now I'm a flashlight," Spot said as she grabbed his tail.

"This is part two of getting through the guards in case anything follows you through the Octaghouls and gets inside the Hedgemaze with you," Isabella said.

"Something could get by those things and in here?" Karah said.

"Don't worry," Isabella said. "Nothing has ever survived the Hedgemaze that's not supposed to."

Karah's face softened when she saw lights at the end of the path and an opportunity to run out of the Hedgemaze. She bumped into Stavvon and Chazz as she did.

"We were on our way to tell you the good news," Stavvon said as he grabbed Karah to keep her from falling.

"Stavvon didn't get in trouble. Shazak did," Chazz said.

"Yeah, the magistrates understood why I had to be careful," Stavvon said. "Shazak has to clean and sweep their offices for two weeks for trying to take someone's candy."

"Even though it was Gigo's," Chazz said.

Karah was relieved and happy for Stavvon, but couldn't get her mind off the Octaghouls or the Hedgemaze. She was especially leery of the Hedgemaze despite the fact that it had angel hair draped all over it. She planned to ask someone to zap her directly to her cottage when the party was over so she wouldn't have to endure the licking again.

When the center of Khalee came into view Karah saw a signpost with four street signs nailed to it that all pointed in the same direction. She wasn't sure where to turn to arrive on Potter's Path, Artesian Avenue, Café Circle, or Tomb Terrace, but Stavvon and Chazz did. They anxiously led the way to Artesian Avenue so she could see Khalee's host of famous painters, writers, musicians, and sculptors. Disappointed when Chopin told her he didn't give autographs because he didn't consider himself more special than anyone else she asked Picasso. To her dismay, she got the same response.

"They were right to decline," Isabella said. "Their special gifts are God at work in them. God's special gifts are at work in everyone. No one has their own ability to do anything."

Karah saw the Route B to Khalee Ferry coast into its docking slip as they turned left onto Tomb Terrace. She ran toward it. Isabella, Stavvon, and Chazz, arrived alongside her in time to watch the captain move to the stern while passengers were unloaded off the bow. She didn't think it strange when he took a white robe and gold belt off and put a black robe and red belt on until he hung a Voyage to the Underworld sign and a man with his hands tied together was escorted aboard.

"The ferry goes to the Underworld?" she said.

"Route Z out of Khalee will get you there," Chazz said.

"Isabella, what did that man do? Did he tell a lie?" she said.

Isabella quickly ushered her troop to the center of Café Circle so Karah would stop thinking about the man the Ferry Captain was taking to the Underworld. Seeing a creature partially wrapped like a mummy outside the Spiritual Warfare Recruiting Office did the trick.

Karah ran to him and read the headline on the newspaper in his hands.

Shazak vs. Stavvon
Verdict
Shazak Sentenced For Sneaking Snacks

"Word quickly goes to print around here too," Karah thought as Isabella borrowed the man's paper so she could read the article.

"Look at the Catlady," Chazz said, pointing toward a little yellow house.

"What Catlady?" Karah said. "All I see are cats everywhere."

There were cats everywhere. Hundreds of them. Sunning themselves on the roof, resting in trees, playing on the porch, perched on windowsills, pawing at fish in a pond, and eyeballing birds bathing in a bathtub in the yard.

"Can't you see her?" Stavvon said. "She's right over there. The woman with a cat head on her left shoulder and a cat head on her right shoulder licking milk out of two saucers of milk."

That Karah saw.

"Her name is Catsidy. She's the CatAngel," Chazz said.

Karah turned toward Stavvon and gave him a grim look.

"If you think that's wild wait till you see beings with three heads," Chazz said.

"Animal or people-like?" Karah said.

"Sometimes a mixture," Stavvon said.

"Both?" Karah said.

"You'll see what I'm talking about when you meet Spike," Stavvon said.

"I just don't want to see anything without a head," Karah said.

"Then you'd better go back to Earth," Chazz said.

"They're teasing, right Isabella?" she said. "Please tell me there are no headless creatures in Khalee."

Stavvon grabbed Karah by her shoulders and turned her around. "There's one right over there," he said.

Karah saw something all right, but the something she saw was no headless creature. The something she saw was the Angel she couldn't wait to meet. "Bettina," she said as she rushed across the street. "My name is Karah. Will you please, please take me with you to arrange the stars sometime?"

"I know who you are," Bettina said. "I heard you wanted to go to work with me. I really shouldn't call it work. It's a blast. I was going to talk to Isabella about it when I saw her at your party."

"My party?" Karah said.

"Do you think Spike's Café is filled at capacity because I'm about to arrive?" Bettina said.

Karah thought, "*Yesssss!*" She couldn't believe she was standing next to the Chief StarAngel. She wanted a picture of Bettina. She wanted her picture taken with Bettina. Better yet, she wanted an autographed picture of Bettina.

"*Now I know why Rabboni doesn't want her to know He's Jesus,*" Isabella thought. "*She'd react to Him as if He was a rockstar, too, instead of focusing on His training.*"

"Can I? Can I please, Isabella?" Karah said.

"I'm sorry," Isabella said. "There's no way you can go out into the cosmos at night."

Karah stared at Bettina trying to will her into changing Isabella's mind.

"I completely agree," Bettina said. "Now is not the time. I will call upon you at Karah's Cottage when the time is right and take you on a spectacular star ride. I promise. Let's go. Everyone is waiting for you inside the café."

Karah was reluctantly ushered inside sporting a dumbfounded expression when she saw half-man, half-woman, half-animal, beings coming at her through perfumed smoke emerging from slitted bowls. "Stavvon I don't know which one of these creatures is your friend Spike, but he's not the only one in here who's an exotic form of the Catlady," she said.

"The invitation must have read: Come One! Come All!" he said.

"Is this wild or what?" Chazz said.

"*Or what?*" Karah thought.

"I didn't think it would be like this," she said as Isabella motioned for Stavvon and Chazz to busy themselves elsewhere.

"I told you they were excited to meet you," Isabella said.

"I mean the creatures," Karah said.

"These are only a sampling of the members of Jesus' Special Forces Units. Most of them aren't here," Isabella said. "They're off patrolling the Universe and the outer limits of the Heavenlies."

Anxious to get to Jesus, Isabella elbowed Karah through the crowd as a man with a ram's head rushed at them shouting, "I'm SirVeyor, Khalee's Facilities Officer. I have blueprints of every abyss and cavity in the Kingdom. If you ever need anything come see me. Drop in anytime. My office is on Tomb Terrace near Rabboni's Office."

Gigo passed them with her nose in the air making sure to keep her distance.

Isabella noticed Karah scowl at her. "That creature over there in the orange and green Hawaiian shirt is Gigo's father," she said.

Karah turned to the counter and scanned all the beings sitting on stools until she came upon the shirt Isabella described. She wasn't surprised he had shark-teeth like his daughter, but she was surprised that they were poking out the top of his head like a drill bit.

"I knew she had shark-blood in her veins," Karah said.

"Don't count her out," Isabella said as she nudged her to keep moving. "No one is beyond being transformed so God can fulfill His plan for them."

Karah started moving, but not fast enough.

Gigo grabbed her arm and said, "My father made me come. Do I look stupid enough to want to come to a party for you?"

Stavvon intervened so Karah could free herself, and apologized to Gigo for accidentally stepping on her foot as he stepped on her foot.

Karah rushed to catch up with Isabella as beings dropped to their knees and began bowing with their hands held high above their heads. "What are they doing?" she said.

"Paying homage to God," Isabella said, "for bringing you to Khalee."

"Have I done something I don't know about?"

"It's not what you've done," Isabella said. "It's what they hope you'll do."

Karah shivered.

Chapter Ten

GET OUT OF THE UNDERWORLD

KARAH LEANED AGAINST a wall in the back of the café to steady herself as the polkadots on a chameleon creature's dress changed from green to purple to red to blue every time a being passed. Seeing Isabella speaking privately with a mysterious man in a corner booth stirred her brains even more. Captivated, she studied his powerful gaze sensing a presence filled with intense strength. She hoped it was Rabboni and that she would also be able to chat with Him so she could get some answers to her many questions. She got her wish when Isabella motioned for her to approach.

Rabboni purposefully remained silent as Isabella put Karah in a chair in front of Him. He wanted her to soak up the look in His eyes that were speaking for Him. He even refrained from smiling as she glanced at an elegantly carved wood box on the table wondering if it was a gift for her. When He was ready to begin He said, "Root beer floats for all."

Karah straighten her back against her chair as the café broke loose with roaring shouts of delight. Those weren't the first words she expected to hear from such a man, but she wasn't surprised He knew root beer floats were her favorite treat.

Thrilled that Rabboni placed an order for the entire café Spike jumped over his serving counter. Karah's eyes swirled as the composite of a dog's head, bottom, and tail, and a man's arms and legs tattooed with depictions of ogres approached the table wearing a spiked collar and ram's horns for ears.

"Where's he going to get vanilla ice cream and root beer to pour over the top?" she wondered as he wiped his hands on his apron.

In that instant, an enormous root beer float appeared in her hands while others like it began floating around the room on invisible serving trays so the crowd of creatures could help themselves.

"Did you already forget about all the wonderful treasures conjured up for your pleasure since you arrived? Even Spot could create everything you wanted," Rabboni said with a lift of his brow as He rose out of his chair.

The café obediently hushed itself in response.

Isabella hurried for the door and said, "Au Revoir. Have to run for a bit. Be here when I get back."

Karah wanted to run after Isabella, but felt supernaturally pressed to her chair. She suddenly feared Rabboni and was sure He was about to proclaim her stupidity for all until He said, "Who would like to attend boot camp with Karah?"

As Stavvon and Chazz shouted, "We would, Sir," with great purpose Rabboni raised His pointing finger at Gigo and said, "You, too! My office, tomorrow morning, 9:00 a.m. sharp."

Karah's heart sank at the same time Gigo's did. "Please don't make her train with me," she said as Gigo glared at her from across a cafe table. "I don't mind going to boot camp with only Stavvon and Chazz. Really I don't."

"I want her to attend with you," He said as He lowered Himself into

His chair. "You can't learn in a bubble. You need to mix with others so you can learn as much as you can as quickly as you're able."

"I can't think of a thing I want to learn from her," she thought.

"I can think of a lot of things I want you to learn from her," He said.

Karah slumped in her chair thinking she would never get used to the fact that nearly everyone in Khalee could read her mind.

"If you're worried about us knowing what you're thinking," Rabboni said, "learn to control your thoughts. Fortunately for you, mastering your thoughts is one of many things I'm going to personally teach you how to do."

"Did you read Gigo's mind? Is she mad at you?" Karah said.

"Don't concern yourself with what Gigo is or isn't," Rabboni said.

"Will she show up tomorrow?" she said.

"What I say goes," He said.

"But what will happen if she doesn't?" she said.

"I said Gigo is none of your concern. Now, forget about her for the moment. I want to show you something," He said.

A serpent-shaped game board appeared on the table with HIDEOUS IT's portrait on one of the spaces as He reached for the elegantly carved box she'd been wondering about. "I created this game for you. It's called *Get Out of the Underworld.* These are the playing pieces," He said as he opened the box and thirty miniature warriors leapt out swinging swords, knives, lances, bows, hatchets, traps, and snares.

Karah jumped out of her chair.

"Sit down," Rabboni said. "They're only getting warmed up so they'll be prepared for the Underworld if their player falls through a slit in the serpent's back. Would you like to play?"

"I don't think so," she said.

"They won't hurt you," He said. "Pick a playing piece. Which one do you want to be yours?" He said.

"I couldn't imagine," she said.

"Then I'll pick for you. You look like a Jacinta player. She sets traps for thieves and liars. Don't drop her," He said as He set Jacinta in her hand. "She might turn out to be one of the best friends you'll ever have."

"Can I put her down?" Karah said. "I think she wants to run around with her little critter friends."

"Yes, while I teach you the rules," He said as He handed her a little book.

Karah read along as Rabboni recited each word:

1. Roll the dice to see how many spaces you get to move across the serpent's back.
2. Land on the symbol for the Trinity you get three Stand Up For Yourself Scripture Cards.
3. Land on the symbol for God you get one Stand Up For Yourself Scripture Card.
4. Land on the symbol for Jesus you get one Stand Up For Yourself Scripture Card.
5. Land on the symbol for the Holy Spirit you get one Stand Up For Yourself Scripture Card.
6. Land on Queen Alexia's crown you get to move forward two spaces.
7. Land on the picture of Isabella you get to more forward one space.
8. Land on the empty bowl you win a refreshing treat.
9. Land on the burning desert, blinding sandstorm, dark corridor or stolen treasure you have to move back two spaces.
10. Land on a sacred animal: the crocodile, lion, beetle, or hippo, you have to put one Stand Up For Yourself Scripture Card back in the pile.
11. Land on a black space (a slit in the serpent's back) you fall into the Underworld and you have to answer a Get Out of the Underworld Question to get back on the game board.
12. Land on fallen Angels: Maleeth or Satan, you get sucked into the Underworld. Landing on one of these evil creatures requires five correct answers to Get Out of the Underworld Questions because they don't let you go without a fight.

13. Land on Ezer you have to answer a Truth Question. The other players get to ask you anything they want. You have to give a truthful answer. If you lie they get to send you to the Underworld forever – You lose – Game over.

14. Land on Progy you earn a Get Out of the Underworld Free Card to be used anytime you choose.

15. For every wrong answer you have to answer two questions correctly. You can only answer Get Out of the Underworld Questions when it's your turn to roll the dice, but you get to keep answering consecutive questions during one turn until you're out of the Underworld or give a wrong answer.

16. When you get out of the Underworld you start over at the beginning on the first square of the serpent's back.

17. The person with the most Stand Up For Yourself Scripture Cards in the end wins.

"This sounds like more than just a game," Karah said. "What are Stand Up For Yourself Scriptures?"

"Spiritual warfare swords. The Bible is like an armory, it's full of them," Rabboni said. "Each scripture contains the Spirit of God. I'll be teaching you how to wield them against Satan. Are you ready to play?"

Karah hurriedly shook her head as the playing pieces struggled with their opponents over their weapons and tried to knock each other off the edge of the table. "This game should be called War," she said.

"Life is a war," Rabboni said. "A Holy War between darkness and light. The answers to the questions illuminate the mind. They teach how God's light destroys Satan's darkness."

"It all sounds so real," she said. "Are the questions hard? If I fall into the Underworld will I be able to get out?"

"The questions aren't hard. They aren't easy either. They're not meant to be. Each one is designed to teach you how and what to think about. The answers are in this," He said, holding out His hands.

Karah sat wondering what Rabboni was talking about until the biggest, fattest book she'd ever seen appeared on the table in front of her. In that moment, she found the courage to question Him about her deepest concern and said, "Can you tell me why ghastly HIDEOUS IT wanted to kidnap me?"

Rabboni dove like an eagle into the answer. "Your providence is to start a spiritual revival that will not end. Satan and HIDEOUS IT want to make sure you never fulfill your purpose. Under My tutelage you'll learn spiritual warfare tactics. Your proving ground will take place in the Underworld where you'll do battle with Satan himself. That's why I created this game. It will teach you how to break free from the grip of demonic influences."

"No way!" Karah said as she jumped out of her chair and knocked her root beer float over. "I can't do what you just said."

"Yes, you can. Spiritual warfare causes demons to run for cover. Merely saying the name of Jesus causes Satan to flee. Now sit down," Rabboni said. "Everyone is staring at you. You will also lower your voice and not use that tone with me."

Karah returned Rabboni's penetrating gaze and did as she was told while Spike handed her a napkin and mopped up her dripping root beer. "Can we talk about this some other time?" she said. "I need to think."

"Yes. Now or later, doesn't matter," He said. "Nothing is going to change. Millions of parents have already asked God to teach their children how to fight spiritual warfare. That person is going to be you."

"They want God. They don't want me. You just said so yourself. They asked God to teach them," Karah said.

"It will be Him. He'll do it through you. He chose you and I'm here to teach you how to surrender your life to Him so He can. The secret is letting go. That's all it takes. When you can do that He'll take you on a road show so children can see how He works in your life."

"Let go! Surrender! That's it! Why are you trying to make it sound easy?" Karah said.

"Letting go is harder than it sounds," Rabboni said, "but it truly is as easy as surrendering. When you develop courageous faith in God through trials and tribulations you'll know you can trust Him. When you know you can trust Him with your life you'll be able to stand strong with Him in any situation."

"I don't want any more trials and tribulations. Wasn't watching my family completely obliterated enough for a lifetime?" she said.

"If you don't get to know God and become stronger through trials Satan and his HIDEOUS IT henchwoman will succeed. They won't even have to lay a hand on you. They're masters at getting people to jump into pits and destroy themselves."

"That'll be me. I'll jump in and self-destruct," Karah said. "I can't survive Satan."

"You're right. You can't, but God's Spirit can. He will equip you to do your part," Rabboni said.

"Even the sound of the word 'Satan' scares me," she said.

"Your destiny is written in God's book. We have all been waiting for you to come of age."

"What age? I'm only twelve," she said. "I can't even drive a car. This doesn't make any sense."

"We each have a purpose. Your's is to become a spiritual warfare warrior. I watched you tell HIDEOUS IT what you thought of her. That took courage. She could have smacked you. This game," He said as He redirected her attention back to the game board, "will teach you how to control your emotions and maintain a sense of peace and order in your mind so you can remain calm and courageous and God can work through you."

"Did my boot camp training start at the rest stop?" Karah said.

"Your training started long, ago," Rabboni said. "Trials help people grow and give God opportunities to prove His faithfulness. You can't develop faith in God without going into battle with Him and you don't ever want to go into any battle without Him."

"Why can't God zap me and fill me with the faith I need?" she said.

"There's an unavoidable process that involves people learning from hardships and failures," He said, "because they were born with a lustful sinful nature; a greedy desire for success; and the prideful need to control their own lives. The only space there is for God in your life is the space you give Him. The more faith you have in Him the more space you'll give Him. The more space you give Him the more powerful He'll become in you. The masses want an ALL powerful God, but they won't give Him time or space to work. They want everything handed to them NOW NOW NOW!"

"Where did God get His powers?" Karah said.

"The only thing you need to concern yourself with is learning how to dance with Him and let Him lead," Rabboni said. "The book I gave you will help you learn your part. It's getting late. You need to go to your cottage and start studying. There's no time to waste. We're going to start playing *Get Out of the Underworld* tomorrow."

"Tomorrow?" Karah said. "This book is huge. It will take forever to read. I won't know any of the answers. I won't be able to get out of the Underworld if I fall into it."

"Ah, perfect timing," He said. "Look who just returned."

Karah filled with relief when she saw Isabella walking through the café with a smile on her face. Rabboni gave her a sit-stay look as He left the table to meet Isabella in the middle of the café. She strained her ears to hear what they were saying, but heard nothing because their mouths didn't move.

Forgetting she was supposed to stay-put she ran after Spot and Aamir as they strutted outside. She wanted some fresh air and hoped to find Stavvon and Chazz so she could talk to them about what Rabboni had told her.

"I've never heard anyone scream so loud in my life," Shazak said when she spotted Karah on the sidewalk.

"That was Gigo," Karah said. "I wasn't the one screaming and it wasn't my candy bag you stuck your snout in."

Isabella rushed out of the café and grabbed Nony and Corissa by their elbows to herd them away from a crowd of beings and said, "Jesus told me we don't have much time to get Karah ready for God's purpose for her. I'm glad it was Him who had to reveal the facts. I couldn't even stay in the café while He did. As expected, He didn't give her an inch of wiggle room. Where is she?" she said as her mind shifted.

"She asked Jasmine to *zap* her to her cottage so she could start reading some big, fat book He gave her," Nony said.

"That big, fat book was a Bible," Isabella said.

"I didn't know," Nony said as Isabella went *poof.*

Chapter Eleven

ROUND ONE - BING!

When Spot leaned in her cottage window and said, "Wakie Wakie," Karah covered her head with her pillow mumbling: "Be still and know that I Am Here. Be still and know that I Am Here." Words carved into her brain the night before. A night with so little sleep she could not recall. Not wanting to even think about her newest, biggest, fattest book she turned over so she couldn't see it on her desk. There was a glitch in her plan. Her pillow vanished and her newest, biggest, fattest book appeared in its place. She was suddenly face down on *The Holy Bible*. That completed her wake up call in a hurry. She flew out of bed with a blanket wrapped around her.

"Good morning," Alexia said, from her mirror throne.

"Good morning," Karah said. "Does Rabboni always do stuff like that?"

"He does have a fun side and a incomparable imagination," Alexia said.

"I'm sure He's written a book about that subject too," Karah said.

"You fit in perfectly in Khalee," Alexia said. "One needs a sense of humor to live in our peculiar corner of the Kingdom."

"I know He's wise," Karah said, "but did He know what He was talking about when He told me I'm going to start a spiritual revival?"

Poof! Alexia vanished leaving Karah wondering if she said something to upset her.

"What's wrong?" Corissa said as she walked in with a box and caught Karah nervously looking about. "Did something happen?"

"No," Karah said, keeping her promise to guard the secret about Alexia. "I'm just tired. I was up all night reading a humongous book Rabboni gave me."

"It's a Bible," Corissa said. "You shouldn't call it pet names."

"What's in there?" Karah said.

"Your boot camp uniform. Isabella sent me out here to give it to you. Put it on so I can pin up your hair."

"I have to wear this?" Karah said as she opened the box.

"Just put it on. It's getting late," Corissa said.

Knowing Karah would appear on her porch wanting to debate having to wear a monk's robe to boot camp Isabella was ready and equipped to distract her with an apple turnover from her favorite patisserie.

Right on cue Karah walked up the steps and said, "Why do I have to wear this? No one will know I'm me. I won't have any friends."

"I don't want anyone to know you're you," Isabella said as she handed her a turnover. "And you can't tell anyone. It's a test for everyone else, to see who can and can't recognize you in disguise."

Things took a turn for Karah when she heard that. She sat down in the porch swing to eat her breakfast. On her first day she was already a trusted insider assigned to play a part in a covert exercise. She smiled and looked down at her cloak, in a different light she saw it much differently. She was proud to be wearing it. She was on her first mission.

"I heard you complaining about some big, fat book Rabboni gave you," Isabella said. "Stop calling it names. It's a Bible. You need to have reverence for it and Rabboni."

"I do respect the Bible and Rabboni," Karah said, "but I'd be lying if I said I'm not upset about all the freaky stuff He told me last night. When I tried to talk to Queen Alexia about it this morning she took off. You do the same thing. Why do you change the subject when I ask you questions?"

"Now for some words of warning before you start your first day," Isabella said.

Karah took a bite of her pastry and rolled her eyes.

"Do not question Rabboni's ways. Do everything exactly as He says. He knows everything. He answers questions with questions to make you think."

"What does God look like?" Karah said. "Can I meet Him?"

"When you study the Bible you'll learn what God expects and how He thinks and operates. When you know these things you will know Him. When you know Him you will be able to feel and sense His spiritual presence and hear His still, small voice - That is how you meet God - You meet Him when you experience Him. When you do it will feel like a face-to-face. You won't need a physical manifestation. His Spirit will be enough.

"You also need to know that God is not separate from you. His Spirit supernaturally arose in you when you accepted Jesus as your Savior. In that moment, He became the oil in your veins that sooths your heart and greases your brains. He operates internally that's why He doesn't need an external audible voice. He stirs believers to act and think and perform from within."

"It's all so confusing," Karah said.

"Ask God to resolve your confusion. He will. He doesn't expect you to understand everything all at once or to be perfect. Let Him be the answer to your every need. When you're faced with something scary pray and recall His past faithfulness and promises. Let Him deal with perpetrators that cause you emotional pain."

"I try but I can't when I'm upset," Karah said.

"I know it's hard to think straight at times, but it's not impossible. It just takes practice," Isabella said as she reached for her dagger and put it in her pocket.

"What's wrong?" Karah said.

"I always lose track of time when I'm talking to you. You need to go. Pull your hood up over your hair," Isabella said.

"Are you taking that to your bank to put in your safe deposit box?" Karah said. "That's where my grampa kept his valuables."

"What? My dagger? Yeah, my safe deposit box."

"I saw a look in your eyes. Did you just tell me a LWL?" Karah said.

"Yes," Isabella said, "but only as a test. We don't have banks or safe deposit boxes in Khalee. Now, will you please stop asking questions and go? You can tell Rabboni you read a LWL in my eyes. He'll be pleased."

"Will He know what that is?"

"You have to ask," Isabella said.

In the middle of her first day of training Karah fell asleep at her desk and woke up screaming. She blathered out an explanation when she saw the looks on Rabboni's, Stavvon's, and Chazz's faces. "I had a nightmare," she said. "It was horrifying. Crazed, snarling horses were stampeding straight toward me carrying ghoulish soldiers."

"Sounds to me like you're the one who's crazed," Gigo said.

"They were wearing helmets and armor," Karah continued. "They jumped off their horses and ran after me. Their Commander was screaming, 'Find her! Find her!' He was dreadful. You know, the killing kind."

"What did he look like?" Stavvon said.

"His face was disfigured plastic. It looked like his flesh had caught on fire, melted, and hardened. His long, black hair was uber greasy and he only had three fingers on his left hand and four on his right.

When he found me hiding under my bed he pulled me out with rubber extender arms. The next thing I knew I was on a pillar in the middle of a ring of fire surrounded by soldiers with bent bows and fiery arrows aimed at me."

Stavvon observed the vivid fear in Karah's eyes knowing Satan released a terrifying brain-bomb in her mind with hopes of discouraging her from accepting God's purpose for her life. He was ready to travel to the Underworld to do battle with him.

Chazz rose out of his chair wishing he could *blink, snap,* and *zap* Karah back to Earth.

Rabboni sent Khalee's Combat Captain a telepathic order to increase His platoon's presence in Khalee and tossed His lesson plan on His desk and said, "Karah, we have a game to start."

"This isn't the time for games," she said. "I want to go back to my cottage."

"What a baby," Gigo said.

"Gigo, you'll be staying to play *Get Out of the Underworld* with Karah. You could use some illuminating," He said.

Stavvon, Chazz, and Aamir caught a get-up-and-leave-look Rabboni threw in their direction. Aamir was hissing all the way out the door. He wanted to stay to see how well Karah could get out of the Underworld and how badly Gigo was going to behave. The door closed and locked itself behind them.

"Let's begin," Rabboni said.

Karah nervously picked up Jacinta when the serpent game board appeared on the table. She rolled the dice, landed on Alexia, and moved forward one space with a sense of satisfaction until Gigo picked out the most vicious warrior in the box. He was clearly ready to play hard. She was sure fire was going to come shooting out the little bugger's nose. Unlike Jacinta, he was the bloodthirsty type.

Her glee returned when Gigo rolled the dice, landed on a slit in the serpent's back, and went straight to the Underworld. *"That's just where you belong,"* she thought as Gigo put her angry fella in the slimy, black hole in the table. Jacinta also smiled a smirky smirk.

Rabboni observed them and tapped His finger on the table to regain their attention. "Gigo," He said, "here's your Get Out of the Underworld question. What is a force-house?"

"The body," she said.

"Correct," He said. "Come out of the Underworld."

Karah straightened in her chair. It was her turn again. She rolled the dice and landed on Progy. "Yea, I get a Get Out of the Underworld Free Card," she said.

Gigo rolled her eyes and grabbed the dice and tossed them. As she moved her warrior everyone could see another slit in the serpent's back in her future. Karah and Jacinta secretly exchanged smiling glances and held their outward composure in check.

"Gigo, here's your Get Out of the Underworld question," Rabboni said. "What's a circular passage?"

"That's easy. A portal," she said.

"Correct," He said. "Come out of the Underworld."

Karah's next turn landed her on a sandstorm. According to the rules she had to move back two spaces as she did she landed on a slit in the serpent's back.

"Look who's in the Underworld now," Gigo said.

"Karah, you have a Progy Card. Do you want to use it to get out of the Underworld?" Rabboni said.

"No," she said. "I don't want to take the easy way out. I want to answer the questions."

"You wish," Gigo said.

"Karah, here's your question," Rabboni said. "What's a chamber?"

"I don't know," she said.

"Your brain you idiot," Gigo said.

Karah was getting sick from having to swallow Gigo's nasty tasting medicine. She didn't want to stop Jacinta from charging across the table to poke the loudmouth with a prong from her snare trap, but she did. She curled her right hand around her and lifted her off the table in a loose fist. They both cooled down when Gigo rolled the dice and landed on another slit in the serpent's back. They didn't gloat for long because they knew she would somehow know the answer to whatever question she was asked.

"Gigo," Rabboni said with an observant eye, "what is the portal of love?"

"The heart," she said.

"Correct," He said. "Come out of the Underworld."

Rabboni turned to Karah, "You now need two correct answers to get out of the Underworld. Are you sure you don't want to use your Progy Card?"

Karah nodded.

Jacinta smiled in agreement even though she was the one who was stuck in the Underworld hole in the table.

"Okay," He said. "Can you tell me how you protect your heart, your portal of love?"

"Don't worry about me," Jacinta said. "I'm proud of you."

"I need an answer," Rabboni said.

"Would you please repeat the question?" she said. "Jacinta was talking."

"She's stalling," Gigo said.

"How do you protect your heart, your portal of love?" Rabboni said.

"I don't know," Karah said.

"I was right. You don't know anything," Gigo said. "You protect your heart by controlling the bad thoughts that get into your brain chamber and make you feel bad."

Fighting tears Karah stared at Rabboni wondering why He wouldn't tell Gigo to behave. She wanted Him to defend her. She wanted Him to banish Gigo and her cold heart forever. She didn't think things could get any worse, but they did. Gigo rolled the dice and landed on the empty bowl. Knowing she'd earned a special treat Karah closed her eyes to avoid her vengeful glare as Rabboni handed her a box of lollipops. Jacinta also turned away.

While Gigo let her wicked little warrior lick the sucker she picked, Rabboni turned to Karah and said, "You now need four correct answers to get out of the Underworld. Are you sure you don't want to use your Progy Card?"

"Yes," Karah said.

"Okay, here's your first question," Rabboni said as Jacinta gave her a thumb-up. "What are precepts?"

"Bible passages," she said with confidence.

"What planet are you from? Are you sure it was Earth?" Gigo said. "They're God's principles that govern actions and conduct."

"So you do know what they are. You choose to disobey," Jacinta said.

Karah was thrilled someone was sticking up for her. It made no sense to her that Rabboni wasn't. She stared at Him in wonder as Gigo rolled the dice and landed on the symbol for Jesus sporting a wide arrogant smile for all to see.

Pretending to not notice, Rabboni said, "Gigo, according to the rules you get to take one Stand Up For Yourself Scripture Card from the pile."

Returning His attention to Karah, He said, "You now need six correct answers to get out of the Underworld. Is it time to use your Progy card?"

"No," Karah said. "I got myself into this mess. I'll get myself out."

"Very, good," Rabboni said.

Gigo was also struck by Karah's commitment to get herself out of the Underworld, but refused to let on.

"Okay, Karah. Here's your first question," He said. "What are fretters?"

"Nervous twitches," she said.

"Close, but not!" Gigo said. "This is more fun than I thought it was going to be. Fretters are fears. Fears cause Earthlings to nervously twitch and twist in their chairs the way you are right now."

Jacinta could no longer restrain herself. She didn't care that Rabboni was there or that she'd get in trouble. She jumped out of the Underworld hole and charged across the table toward Gigo. Karah didn't stop her this time. She encouraged Jacinta by smiling when she pinched Gigo. They then both cheered as Gigo landed on Ezer knowing she was going to have to truthfully answer a question or go to the Underworld for good. Gameover!

"Karah, ask Gigo a question," Rabboni said, after letting her think a moment.

Jacinta was also anxiously waiting.

"Why are you so mean?" Karah said.

"Because it's fun to watch people like you get upset," Gigo said.

Karah popped out of her chair shouting, "GAME OVER! LIAR! I'm sure you do think it's fun to be mean, but the truth is you're mean because you locked God out of your cold, bitter heart so He can't defrost you and keep you from acting like a SheDemon."

"We're done for today. Gigo you can go," Rabboni said.

Gigo couldn't get out the door fast enough.

"What are you smiling about?" Karah said.

"Your analysis," Rabboni said. "That comment about God being locked out of Gigo's heart made all the Archangels in Khalee smile. You illuminated Gigo's core issue. You saw the affects of quenching God's Spirit and shined God's light on it. You shouldn't have lost control and yelled, but that's okay. You're a work in progress. You always will be."

"She's awful. Why are you letting her be mean?" Karah said.

Karah took the words right out of Jacinta's mouth. She, too, wanted to know why Rabboni was being overly tolerant with Gigo. She, too, had her hands on her hips, but she was also tapping her foot on the table.

"Besides that," Karah said, "you told me the questions weren't going to be hard. Jacinta and I are going to be stuck in the Underworld forever. It's embarrassing. I studied all night. I still couldn't answer one stupid question."

"The combined answers to all the questions will one day save your life. Do not call them stupid," Rabboni said.

"I'm sorry," she said. "The truth is I'm upset because I have to play with Gigo. What's the point if she, she, she makes it impossible for me to think straight? If I can't think I can't learn."

"That's your problem not Gigo's and one you need to fix," Rabboni said. "She has no control over you unless you give it to her. You're playing with her so you can learn to think under pressure. Think of Gigo's words as fretters you need to capture and toss out of your mind. You need to become deaf to them. You need to learn how to play with her without getting upset."

"Can you tell me why Gigo is allowed to be a Warrior in Training?" she said. "Even Stavvon and Chazz think she's a DIT."

"What is or isn't tolerated and why is God's business. He has His reasons. Would you like Him to give up on you the way you think everyone should give up on Gigo?" He said.

Karah slumped in her chair ashamed of herself.

"You're forgiven," He said. "You have a lot to learn about how to feel and react when people are hurtful. I know that. Everyone in the Kingdom knows how you feel and that dear child is why you're here. Our mission is to teach you to think the way God does and to extend grace and compassion to others as I did you. Do you want to be pleasing to God?"

Karah nodded.

"Then start responding to Gigo with God's grace and mercy. Show Him you can win a war over your mind by not acting the way she does and by not letting her get under your skin the next time you girls play *Get Out of the Underworld*."

"There's going to be a next time?" she said.

"There will always be a next time with someone or something," Rabboni said. "Gigo is your training partner this time around. When you stop letting her push your buttons you won't have to play *Get Out of the Underworld* with her anymore. Let that be your motivation. I do have one more question to ask before you go. Is there room in your cottage for an overnight guest? Jacinta wants to go home with you."

Chapter Twelve

FLAPPING OUT OF HIS MIND

JACINTA HAPPILY JIGGLED in the palm of Karah's hand until they spotted a horse drawn circus wagon in the distance. She shouted for Karah to stop when she ran toward it, but she wouldn't listen. She was too enticed by the colorful painting of an exotic lion on the outside. She'd only seen pictures of circus wagons in books. She wanted to meet the driver and see if he had an amazing creature chained up on the inside.

The circus wagon did have a fascinating creature inside - A jolly giant of a man whose eyes went in different directions: One looked left while the other looked right, but he wasn't chained up. He jumped out of the backend without warning and nearly landed on top of her. She began slowly withdrawing hoping he could only see in easterly and westerly directions and wouldn't notice her heading south, but the big-ox-sized man reached for her. "Please don't hurt me," she said as his hand landed on her shoulder.

"Is nots gonnas hurts yas, littles Ms. Is sorrys. Is didnts means tas scares yas. Is mustas givens yas a frights jumpins downs likes thats. Wouldnts haves ifs Is seens yas comins. Mes names Flapps. Mes reals names Victors, buts peoples onlys calls mes Flapps. Donts knows whys thats tis. Is a Spices Traders. Is gots a wagons fulls. Is alsos gots a wagons fulls ofs olives. Is nearlys drownins ins ems Is gots so manys. Likes a plagues a frogs theys justs keeps comins. Bless thos Is feels. Comes takes a peeks. Is gots Wilds Turkeys, Asians Horses, Camels Eyes, Bisons Dungs, Musks Tusks, ands Amurs Tigers shavings. Chooses yours owns poisons."

What stopped Karah from turning tail and leaping into the nearest tree was Flapp's one merry eye that told her he didn't have the slightest clue about what it meant to be harmful. She was also charmed by his sincere smile that he showed off as he bent over to tie what was left of his broken shoelaces. It was, however, his sweet apology that caused her to speedily jump into his wagon and smell the contents of a bottle through its filmy wrap. "Yuck! Where'd you get this?" she said.

"Thats theres Bisons Dungs. Fews lives tas tells abouts thats ones afters takins a swifs sniffs ins thes noses likes yers justs dids," Flapp said.

"I wish I had some of that for trap bait," Jacinta said. "Evil loves the smell of evil."

"Is knows hows ta shares littles ones," Flapp said as he put a pinch of his Bison Dung in Jacinta's armor pocket. "Is gots thats spices nears thes Borderlands. Its freshs. Yas has mes words. Is wus outs theres yesterdays tils Is runs intos a gatherins of whats lookeds likes spies. Ids stills bes outs theres buts nows mes ons a treasures hunts."

"For what?" Karah said.

"A tots. Is hads a visions abouts a bunchs a soldiers ridings ups to mes, buts its wus mores thans a visions. Theys spokes tos mes sayings theys offerings a rewards fors a littles girls thats ins Khalees. Nows Is checkings froms houses tas houses lookins fors thes tots."

"A reward for a little girl?" Jacinta said. "What's her name?"

"Whats is hers names? Hmmmms? Can'ts remembers," Flapp said as he scratched his head. "Alls Is knows is hers gots pigtails."

Karah slowly lowered herself onto the seat of his wagon barely able to breathe as Flapp picked Jacinta up and placed her on his knee. She was relieved Corissa had pinned her pigtails up on the back of her head. She looked at her monk robe sleeves knowing the truth about why she was wearing a disguise.

Jacinta watched Karah hoping she wasn't going to suddenly bolt out of the wagon. She didn't want a hasty exit to tip Flapp off even though she seriously doubted his ability to make any sort of connection between his ears. *"We'll wait,"* she told herself. *"Nothing is going to happen to Karah, not on my watch. I'll keep him flapping, find out everything I can, and gradually work her out of the wagon."*

"That sounds fascinating," Jacinta said with a forced smile. "Please go on. We want to hear every juicy detail. Did they tell you why they're looking for her?" she said.

"Theys didnts tells mes," Flapp said. "Is hasnts founds hers. Ohs, yous cans tells Is donts gots hers cants yas? Buts Is wills. Yeps. Das soldiers tolds mes shes causeds quites a stirs."

"Do tell," Jacinta said. "What'd she do?"

"Is askeds buts das mans ons das horses tolds mes its werents anys ofs mes biznis. Hes justs tolds mes hes gives mes servants tas dos mes cookins and cleanins and a bags o'coins ifs Is brings hers tos hims. Is gots tas says hes lookeds a mights crazeds. Yas haves familys?" he said as his mind shifted. "Anys sisters? Is sevens. Guess thats whys Is a drifters. Is coulds always hears ems creepins arounds diggins ins eachs others drawers goins snoops, snoops, snoops. Wells thats whats girl-sisters dos, donts theys?"

Knowing Flapp had run out of sense and information, Jacinta pretended to look at a nonexistent watch on her wrist and motioned it was time for her and Karah to be going.

Oblivious to Jacinta's hint Flapp kept flapping. "Is bloods rights tas greats wealths. Is hasnts founds its," he said, holding up empty hands. "Thats whys Is gots tos sells olives and spices tils Is finds das tots thats comes withs a rewards. Hers mays bes mes tickets tos mes pots-o-golds. Its a bits winds chillys fers a summers days aints its?"

While Flapp's brains continued leaking out his mouth Jacinta ran her hand over her face thinking her brains were going to explode. Aamir's brains already had. He was about to completely implode as he slithered up to the wagon that in his opinion had a dunce for a driver and a very, foolish Karah inside. When he couldn't take anymore of Flapp's flap he started hissing, "Littleeeee Missyyyyyy, whatttttt dooooooo youuuuuu thinkkkkkk youuuuuu areeeeee doingggggg innnnnn thatttttt wagonnnnnnn?"

Karah shot out of her seat knowing Aamir's longer than usual hissy words meant she was in more trouble than usual. She promptly decided to pretend she had a good reason for being in the wagon. She threw open the canvas flap, looked over the side, put on a winning grin, and said, "Hi Aamir. This is Flapp. He has a wagon full of olives. Do you think Isabella would like some?"

"Isabellaaaa knowssss thatssss notttt whyyyy youuuu gottt innnn thatttt wagonnnn. Getttt outtttt, rightttt nowwww," he said.

Flapp's knees went weak when he saw a cobra with swirling fluorescent eyeballs glaring at him and Karah. At that moment he wanted her out of his wagon as much as Aamir did. He lifted her by her armpits, lowered her to the ground, handed her a complimentary jar of olives, and smiled at Aamir all the while. "Is didnts means tas gets anybodys ins troubles. Is bes goings nows," he said as he climbed into his squeaky wagon seat and grabbed his horse's reins.

"Why'd you scare him away?" Karah said as Flapp drove off. "He's a nice man."

"Youuu don'ttt knowww thattt. Youuu can'ttt knowww thattt becauseee he'sss aaa strangerrr," Aamir said.

"That doesn't mean I shouldn't talk to him," she said.

"OHHHHHH YESSSSSS ITTTTTT DOESSSSSS," Aamir said.

Jacinta gave Isabella privacy to reprimand Karah by waiting outside the kitchen door where she could get an eyeful of the legendary sycamore tree trunks. She'd only heard how sinister they looked and wanted to see them up close. She stayed quiet when Karah came out and simply waddled along behind her through the blossoming vines doing her best to keep up.

Karah did need some peace and solitude. Enduring a satanic brain-bomb attack; a vicious battle-game with Gigo; and one of Isabella's infamous-scoldings all in one day amounted to a very, hard day by anyone's standards. Hoping her day would soon end she closed her cottage door. Her expectations were quickly crushed when the miniature warriors left behind in Rabboni's *Get Out of the Underworld* game box came charging out from under her bed with their fangs locked in place and their knives, swords, and other wicked weapons raised. "How'd you get here?" she incredulously said as they challenged her first step. "Why are you mad at me? What did I do?"

"You didn't ask if you could take all of us home with you," their leader said as they inched their way to her feet.

Karah was given no time to reason with her invaders. The next word she heard was *"ATTACK!"* She was thrust into another unimaginable battle. Her big toe received the first stabbing blow. She responded by flicking and swatting at the rodent like creatures scurrying around her feet.

Stavvon and Chazz arrived at her door in time to hear the first loud 'Ouch.' They also heard jumping, thumping, leaping, and tumbling accompanied by nasty snarls, hisses, and growls. When Isabella appeared they all ran to Karah's window to see what was going on. Their smiles grew wide when they saw a miniature battle taking place on her rug.

"Perfect job for you boys. I stopped playing with toy soldiers years ago," Isabella said as she strutted back to her house.

Filled with excitement Stavvon and Chazz clambered over her windowsill and into her cottage shouting, "How beautiful the battlefield."

Karah jumped out of their way and backed into a wall shaking her head in amazement. She hadn't seen them this excited since they dove into *Route B to Khalee* on their bikes. In the midst of all the action she concluded that boys, even Warrior In Training Boys, will be boys.

"We need a shoebox," Stavvon said as he tossed Karah's favorite sandals on the floor.

"Shazam. You got one," Chazz said when he saw a bearded warrior crimped up in a corner wearing a defeated look.

"I didn't want to hurt him. I had to. He was like a pitbull," Karah said, pointing at her ankle. "The only way I could get him off was to smack him. That's the only reason he hit the wall. I swear."

"Don't worry," Chazz said. "These little peeps aren't on the sacred list."

Karah looked at Queen Alexia and saw her laughing from her mirror throne with an oriental fan partially covering her face. She could only see her eyes, but there was no doubt she was thoroughly amused.

Struck by a sudden idea, Karah grabbed a bottle of perfume and sprayed it over the mini-warriors' heads hoping it would slow them down. It worked. The weakened, blurry-eyed, stumbling creatures started dropping their weapons.

Stavvon and Chazz didn't wait to see if their leader was going to pull a white flag out of his armour and formally surrender his troop. They plucked them off the floor and tossed them in the shoebox.

"Did you get them all?" Karah said.

"How many are there supposed to be?" Stavvon said.

"Thirty, including Jacinta," she said.

Chazz emptied another shoebox.

With a box full of steel plated critters in one hand Stavvon transferred them one-by-one into Chazz's empty box as they both counted them. Karah hovered over their shoulders double checking their math. The transfer ended on count twenty-eight.

"One's missing," Jacinta said.

Without delay they began searching for the last little soldier. Jacinta crawled under Karah's closet, bed, and desk. Karah pulled her bed apart to look under the covers. Stavvon searched on top of every piece of furniture and checked inside the closet to make sure it wasn't hanging onto one of her togas by its teeth. Chazz headed for her drinking fountain room after carefully removing the books from the shelves.

After her cottage was thoroughly tossed, Karah had another brilliant idea and said, "Jacinta put some of the Bison Dung Spice that Flapp gave you on the rug."

The smell of the bait permeated the room as Jacinta pulled a pinch from her pocket.

"What stinks?" Chazz said.

"It's the Bison Dung Spice," Karah said. "I'm hoping the odor will draw the trickster out."

It did. They all watched the sneaky sprite sniff its way out of Karah's backpack and head straight for Jacinta. When Karah sensed it was thirsting for the evil smelling treats in Jacinta's hand, instead of the pinch she'd placed on the floor, she waited to see what it was going to do before taking action. As the mini-warrior made its intentions clear by raising its hatchet over Jacinta's head Karah made her intentions clear in return and raised her foot over its head and said, "I don't want to hurt you but I will if you don't drop that hatchet on the floor."

The critter lowered its weapon and got down on one knee.

Stavvon was impressed. He also got down on one knee to show the little soldier some dignity and held the box filled with captured critters to the floor so it could proudly march inside on its own.

"This cottage is now an uninhabitable disaster area," Isabella said as she appeared in the window wearing green facial goo. "Does anyone know someone who might have a magic wand? It's going to take one to clean up the mess you kids made."

"If you find anyone with one of those please ask them to turn my sandals into Army boots. My toes feel like pincushions. I was joking," Karah said as black steel toed boots appeared on her feet. "I'm not wearing these."

Chapter Thirteen

SWORD OF SILENCE

"All of you. Go into the wild in search of one force that has two opposing forces. An offensive force and a defensive force. Come to class tomorrow with a two-page report," Rabboni said.

"The answer will come to you, Karah," Stavvon said as they filed out of Rabboni's office.

Gigo was fuming as she picked up her bike. Nature and exercise were dirty words to her. She was even angrier when Progy rolled up to Karah so she could simply climb onto him. Her resentment intensified when Stavvon and Chazz wheeled off through the swirling morning mist close behind her as if she was a universal treasure.

Karah cycled through the wild with Aamir in her basket pondering Rabboni's question. *"How can one force have two opposing forces? The answer will 'come' to me. What did Stavvon mean?"* she wondered. She asked God if He would please reveal the answer to Rabboni's question of the day and began watching for it. She saw moist pine needles collect on her bicycle tires while steering through colonies of snails. She was sure they didn't have opposing forces. She listened to the rhythmic chatter of songbirds perched on Aamir until he hissed at them for poking him with their claws. When they continued chirping as they flew away she didn't sense opposing forces within them. She witnessed spiders showing off the intricate weavings of their webs as if they were arts and crafts for sale. *"Unless they're poisonous they also don't have the opposing forces Rabboni expects me to discover,"* she thought.

It was sometime before anyone spoke and when someone did it was Gigo. Her silence breaking words were of course snotty, but she went back to being silent when no one responded. Now, that Karah felt and heard. Everyone's silence caused Gigo to go back to being silent. Her silence was so silent it was shouting: 'Here I am I'm silence.' An understanding smile took hold when she sensed a glimmer of what the answer to Rabboni's question might be and realized she could use silence as a weapon against someone who wanted to argue with her.

Following the path Stavvon was carving through the woods she found herself dangerously perched on the side of a cliff. A thunderous raging waterfall was gushing over a granite mountaintop, reaching into the clouds on the other side of the canyon.

Gigo came to a stop alongside Stavvon when she realized he intended to lead everyone up a skinny worm-like trail to the top of the falls. "You're crazy if you think I'm going up this way," she said.

Karah didn't like the looks of the trail either. It was footpath narrow. To make matters worse the moss covered steppingstones were made slippery from overspray rising from trillions of tons of water crashing without mercy into the canyon. "Stavvon are you sure about this?" she said.

Seizing an opportunity to show Karah up, Gigo rose above her own fear and said, "It's safe. Get out of my way," as she squeezed passed Stavvon to take the lead.

Karah's eyes went over the side and locked on the river snarling like vicious storm clouds.

"Don't look down," Stavvon said.

"You won't have to tell me twice," she said as she regained her balance.

Soon there was as much silence on the path leading up the falls as there had been on the trail leading to it. This time the silence was so everyone could concentrate on every step they took. Karah felt and heard that, too. It was an opposing force of the one she'd experienced earlier. She now knew that silence has two opposing forces: The kind one can use on him or herself as opposed to the kind one can use on someone else.

She filled with glee knowing she was going to be able to tell Rabboni she discovered the answer to His question. She planned to tell Him she liked both forces and knew how to use them. *"In my paper,"* she mused, *"I'll illustrate how one can use silence like a double-edged sword and cut through him or herself with one side or through someone with the other. I'll title my report The Sword of Silence."*

When the path widened Gigo stopped being cautious and quickly went from being filled with arrogant pride to being filled with terrifying regret as she went over the side shrieking and frantically grabbing for something to hold onto.

Karah, Stavvon, and Chazz jumped off their bikes and rushed to the edge of the cliff to grab her hands, hoping to keep her from falling to the canyon floor. This time the sounds and forces of the atmosphere didn't make Karah feel like she was being supernaturally sucked over the side.

When Stavvon and Chazz had Gigo securely in their grips Karah ran to get Aamir out of Progy's basket and returned with a stiff Aamir-stick. She snagged Gigo's belt loop with the crooked tip of his tail and said, "Stavvon and Chazz count to three and pull while I lift."

Eureka, Gigo was back on the path. She got there by flying like a bird, but she didn't land like one. She went thud.

Chazz started laughing, thinking she looked like a turtle on its back when she couldn't turn over.

Progy sent his wheels spinning in the background.

Aamir enjoyed the sight as well.

Stavvon also thought the vision of Gigo trying to fly with her arms and legs flapping was funny, but he didn't laugh knowing how she was going to react once she got on her feet. He helped her up and filled with relief when she only grabbed her bike and stormed up the trail.

Karah didn't laugh either. She was worried. She knew Gigo to be the type to get back at them by looking for and finding a place on the trail where she could ambush them. Even so, she still felt nothing but courage when she picked Progy up to finish the steep climb. She had conquered her fear of the side of the cliff. She felt tall, very tall, and capable for the first time in her life. She was refreshed with newly found fearlessness acquired by learning how to survive in the wild and by accepting alternative ways of thinking and doing things.

Karah was growing, but she still didn't want to get chummy with Gigo. She avoided her when she rode off the trail at the top of the falls. She parked Progy next to a footbridge where she discovered quiet, smooth water that appeared motionless. It wasn't. It was a very, deep funnel of water feeding the raging waterfall.

"Jump in and take a swim," Gigo said.

Unbeknownst to Gigo Stavvon was walking up to the tree she was sitting under and heard her tempt Karah into taking a deadly plunge. He'd had enough. He snapped and said, "Karah helped keep you from falling into bone crushing rapids. You should be thanking her. What's your problem?"

When she heard the exchange Karah felt the need to apologize to Gigo for their various reactions to her embarrassing mishap on the trail. She walked over to where she and Stavvon were staring each other down and said, "We weren't laughing at you or about what happened. It truly wasn't funny. It just looked funny. It would have looked funny if it had happened to me, but we were wrong to laugh. Please accept my apology."

Stavvon and Chazz were stunned by Karah's sincere expression of remorse in the face of Gigo's recent death swim taunt.

"Us to," Stavvon said as Chazz nodded.

"Get away from me. I'm outta here," Gigo said.

"What's with her?" Karah said. "I said what I felt God wanted me to say and she got mad."

"Doesn't matter," Chazz said. "You did what you were supposed to do. We're supposed to treat other people right regardless of how they treat us."

"That doesn't make us weak," Stavvon said. "It takes strength to not respond in kind when someone is mean and nasty. We can't lower our behavior standards just because someone else does. We're supposed to control our emotions and actions."

"Mouthing off or hitting back is easy," Chazz said. "Rising above rejection, abuse, and betrayal is hard. It takes a very, secure person to walk away and let someone think they got away with something. People who can do that are those who know God is going to deal with their perpetrators in ways they can't."

"Which is why we're supposed to pray for people who hurt us," Stavvon said, "and why we're supposed to forgive and apologize even if someone doesn't accept it. Ignore Gigo, no matter what she says or does. She's God's problem not our's."

"Same goes for Satan," Chazz said. "No matter what he says or does to mess you up, He's God's problem not your's. God is watching and listening. When the time is right He will free you from Satan's attempts to block you and turn you into damaged goods."

"What you discovered today should help you ignore Gigo and block evil thoughts and negative impressions that knock your emotions around," Stavvon said. "You did discover the force with two opposing forces, didn't you?"

"Yes, I did. Your silence screamed the answer. I now know how to use the external kind of silence on people trying to cut through me and the internal kind when I need to cut through myself."

When Stavvon and Chazz began strangely staring at her she became uncertain.

"Is that wrong?" she said.

"No, you got it right," Stavvon said.

"Then what's with the looks?" she said.

"Rabboni just informed us we're excused from training tomorrow," Stavvon said. "My guess is you're going to be playing *Get Out of the Underworld* with Gigo."

"Oh, no, poor Jacinta. What am I talking about? Poor me," Karah said.

Chapter Fourteen

ROUND TWO – BONG! BOOM!

KARAH STEERED PROGY into an alley to avoid Gigo when she saw her leaning against a building and came close to running over SirVeyor. Quickly veering to her right she came to an abrupt stop outside his office. "I'm sorry I almost hit you," she said.

"I saw what happened," he said. "Can you tell me why Gigo's presence caused your mind to spin."

"I've never been alone with her before," she said.

"You weren't," he said. "You have God and Jesus for bookends, the Holy Spirit inside you, and you're riding around on the Prince of Guardian Creatures. That's four Protectors. Isn't that enough?"

"I wasn't thinking," she said as the realization hit her.

"You got scared and forgot, didn't you?" he said.

Karah nodded.

"Being frightened is a natural reaction when someone greets you in an uncivilized manner," SirVeyor said. "Not that I've ever been frightened. I can imagine why you were, but what does that tell you?"

"That I still don't know how to think under pressure," she said.

"Yes. Now, please come inside and have a cup of hot chocolate and visit with me for a while," he said.

"I can't. I'm on my way to Rabboni's office for *Master Your Thoughts* training," she said.

"Then I'll walk with you and Progy. I want to talk to Him, too," he said.

"About me being afraid of Gigo?" she said.

"No," he said.

"What do you want to talk to Him about?" she said.

"Top Secret Stuff," he said. "Rabboni will know what it all means."

"*All?*" Karah thought.

"Sorry for the delay. Let's get started," Rabboni said as He escorted SirVeyor out the back door of His office. "Put your warriors on the game board where they were when Round One ended. Karah that means Jacinta is in the Underworld and you need to answer six questions to get her out. Have you given anymore thought to using your Progy Card?"

"No, I mean yes," she said. "I've thought about it. I still want to get out on my own."

Gigo couldn't believe her ears, yet she did.

"Very well, Karah." Rabboni said. "Here's your first question."

"What are chains that bind?"

"Ah, ah, ah," she said.

"Here we go again," Gigo said. "They're fretters. Chains that bind the mind are fretters. You probably forgot what fretters are too. They're fears. Your many, many frightful fears."

Jacinta struggled to restrain herself from jumping out of the Underworld with her fists drawn.

"Rabboni, I've been studying. I really have," Karah said.

Gigo groaned, rolled her eyes and the dice, moved her warrior six spaces, and smiled when she landed on Isabella.

"Gigo, according to the rules," Rabboni said, "you get to move forward one space."

"Karah," Rabboni said, "you now need eight correct answers to get out of the Underworld. Are you going to use your Progy Card?"

"I can't. I need to start getting the answers right," Karah said.

"I agree," He said. "Can you tell me how one hears?"

"Only when they listen. Not everyone listens," Jacinta whispered.

"They're cheating," Gigo said.

"I didn't ask Jacinta to tell me the answer," Karah said.

"I know. Here's another question," Rabboni said. "What are Swords of Light?"

"I know the answer, I just can't remember the word for it," she said.

"That makes no sense," Gigo said. "If you can't remember the word you don't know the answer. Swords of Light are scriptures. All the scriptures in the Bible are spiritual warfare swords."

Gigo rolled the dice and landed on a crocodile.

"Landing on a crocodile means you have to put a Stand Up For Yourself Scripture Card back on the pile," Rabboni said.

"Like I need them," she said.

"If you only knew how much," Jacinta said.

"Karah, you now need ten correct answers to get out of the Underworld," Rabboni said. "I'm going to stop asking if you want to use your Progy Card."

"It's about time," Gigo thought.

"Karah, your being is three-fold," Rabboni said. "What are the three-folds? This is a three-point question. If you get this right you'll be three steps closer to getting out of the Underworld."

Karah hesitated and turned her head to one side so she could concentrate.

"Come on we don't have all day," Gigo said.

Karah didn't respond. She remained deep in thought. *"It's my fault if I can't think around Gigo,"* she reminded herself. *"I must think. I must remember to ignore bullies and thugs and let God deal with them."*

"Hurry up and answer the question," Gigo said. "Your time is almost up."

Karah still didn't react.

Rabboni happily watched Karah maintain her composure and turn a deaf ear to Gigo. He was very, pleased.

Jacinta was also relieved to see how calm and collected Karah was becoming. She slowly and quietly repeated the question for her, "You are three-folds. What are the three-folds of your being?"

"Spiritual, Mental, and Physical," Karah said.

"Yahooooooo," Jacinta said.

"Excellent," Rabboni said. "You now only need seven correct answers to get out of the Underworld. Here's another three-pointer. How is power given away?"

"By relinquishing it, by quitting, and by giving in to sin," she said.

"Only four more to go and we'll be back on the game board," Jacinta said.

"Karah," Rabboni said, "what happens when you relinquish your power to someone?"

"They use it on you," she said, looking straight at Gigo.

Unable to control her excitement Jacinta cut loose shaking her traps over her head while shouting, "Three! Three! That's all we need! Three! Three! That's all we need!"

Rabboni motioned for Jacinta to settle down as He considered His next question for Karah. "Name one thing that should never prompt a response?" He said.

"Pride."

"Where is freedom found?"

"In God's promises."

"How is freedom obtained?"

"By believing God will keep His promises. I did it. I did it. I'm out of the Underworld," Karah said.

"Whoopee," Gigo said as she rolled the dice. "I landed on Progy. Now I have a Get Out of the Underworld Free Card just like Karah."

Karah rolled the dice, moved Jacinta six spaces, and landed on a slit in the serpent's' back.

Gigo burst out laughing.

"Karah," Rabboni said as Jacinta plopped back into the Underworld hole, "are darkness and light in the same place?"

"No," she said.

"You're an imbecile!" Gigo said. "The answer is yes. They're both in your mind warring it out with each other."

Jacinta sent one of her traps flying across the table. It didn't help the situation. Gigo laughed even louder when her warrior player snagged it in midair and flung it back at her.

"Gigo's right," Rabboni said as He held up His hands to impose a truce. "Darkness is in your mind where light is. When you focus on fretters (fears) that get into your chamber (mind) they form a darkness that can smother God's Light. Do you now see how all the questions I've been asking are aimed at showing you what your mind can do 'for' you and 'to' you?"

"This is boring," Gigo said.

"Gigo you just caused yourself to land on a slit in the serpent's back," Rabboni said. "Put your player in the Underworld with Jacinta. You also don't get to answer a 'get out' question until your next turn."

"That's not in the rule book," Gigo said.

"It is now," Rabboni said.

"Fine. Skip me. I don't care. Karah is only going to get her next question wrong and dig another deep hole for herself," she said.

"Karah, here's a two-pointer," Rabboni said. "What is darkness and light?"

"Darkness is evil. Light is good," she said.

"Your turn again, Gigo. We're out of the Underworld," Jacinta said as she popped out of the Underworld hole.

"Gigo are you ready for the first of your five questions," Rabboni said.

"Five!" she said.

"Yes, five," He said. "You mouthing off about being bored by My explanation of the Swords of the Light Words was equal to landing on Maleeth or Satan and getting sucked into the Underworld."

113

"Talk about deep holes," Jacinta said while jiggy-jig dancing on the table.

"Gigo, what does Transmutation mean?" Rabboni said as He motioned for Jacinta to stop.

"Transmutation?" she said. "What kind of word is that?"

"I know what it means," Karah said. "Transmutation occurs when the light in one's mind shines on darkness and turns disorder into order."

Gigo let out a wicked laugh that would remove the bark from a dog.

Jacinta scowled at her and said, "What's so funny? Karah was right."

"Karah is and so are you," she said. "You're both losers."

When Jacinta lost control and shouted charge Rabboni lifted her off the table by the back of her armor. Her legs were kicking in the air as Karah calmly got out of her chair, crossed over to Gigo's side of the table, looked at Rabboni, and said, "Can the game be over?"

Gigo turned stiff upon seeing more of the astonishing change in Karah.

"Yes. The game is over. Gigo you're free to go," Rabboni said. "Karah has released you. You don't have to play *Get Out of the Underworld* any more. Thank you for the part you played in helping her learn how to ignore insults so she can concentrate and create order in her mind."

A red-faced Gigo imploded as stomped toward the door.

"See, I kept My word. I told you when you learned to think around Gigo and could control yourself and answer the questions you wouldn't have to play with her anymore. You proved you can master your thoughts and spit darkness and evil suggestions out of your mind. You get a special prize. Five lollipops. Take one of each flavor," He said as he handed her a bowl full and popped a red one in His mouth.

"Now, I know why Gigo materialized in the cave," Karah said, "and why you made her go to boot camp with me."

"Who else could I put you in the ring with?" He said. "You can't develop spiritual muscles unless you workout with heavyweights. I allowed her to be nasty to facilitate your training."

"Did I earn an early release, too?" she said.

"Yes, but only for today. Come tomorrow with Stavvon and Chazz. I have something very, special planned for all of you." Considering something else He wanted to make sure she understood He said, "Karah, will you please answer one more question for me?"

"I'll try," she said.

"Can you tell me what the Trinity is?"

"That's easy. The unity of the three persons of the Godhead: God the father, God the Son (Jesus), and God The Holy Spirit. They're one in the same. Each is God simultaneously performing different functions and roles in their children's lives," she said as she unwrapped a lollipop.

Karah's heart was wildly excited as she jumped on Progy and rode off. Filled with joy her head was high. She was transformed. She felt competent. She felt free of her old-self. She now knew what it felt like to transmute. She'd done it. She'd succeeded at being less of herself and letting God's Spirit control her emotions and reactions. *"Nothing can ever bring me down again. I'm bigger, faster, and stronger now,"* she told herself. She headed Progy toward Spike's hoping to find Stavvon and Chazz until she spotted Gigo waving her down. Wishing she had a wireless remote that would flick her into oblivion she straddled Progy thinking, *"Who sprinkled you with happy dust?"*

"Thanks for waiting for me," Gigo said.

"This isn't me waiting for you," Karah said. "This is me wanting to know what you want."

"I want to tell you I'm sorry for being so mean," Gigo said. "I won't be anymore. I promise. I underestimated you. I thought you were a full-blooded prisspot. You're not. Please forgive me."

Karah stared at Gigo thinking, *"Does she think I'm stupid enough to accept a promise coming from her?"*

"I said I'm sorry. I mean it. I really do," Gigo said. "I don't blame you for not believing me. Let me prove it by taking you to an amazing swimming pond. It's the most beautiful one in all of Khalee and only one of a few that isn't a sacred animal habitat."

Karah remained silent. She didn't believe Gigo, but didn't want to tell her and start an argument. She was also enticed by the vision Gigo described. She continued her silence wondering if she should give her a chance and thought, *"Why am I back to feeling fearful of her? I can now control myself and her. She can't hurt me. I should go and check it out.* Okay," she said. "Progy and I will follow you."

Gigo excitedly began pedaling in a southerly direction along a crooked path. Karah followed. She enjoyed the ride and surprisingly Gigo's company until a fading tremor rippled through her middle and she was whacked on the top of her head by a tree branch. A split second later a boulder came crashing down a mountain toward her. Progy swerved to avoid it. "Let's go back," she said. "Something bad is going to happen."

"Nothing is going to happen," Gigo said. "I would be able to sense it. Besides, we'll be there in a minute."

Karah veered to the left behind Gigo and saw a ditch running alongside the trail. Knowing Progy could keep her safely out of it, she lifted her hands to shade her eyes and saw a paradise pool in the distance. She was delighted to discover it was all Gigo promised. She'd never seen anything as lovely as floating orchids providing perfumed nests for tropical birds to land on. She was also relieved to discover Gigo had been truthful and embraced her previous offer of friendship.

"Let's race to the waterfall," Gigo said.

Knowing she was a very, good swimmer Karah's enthusiasm carried over into eagerly accepting Gigo's spirited challenge. She lowered Progy to the ground, bent over as if she was going to smooth out the wrinkles in her socks, and dove in on the count of three.

Gigo made sure Karah didn't get far. She took aim and purposefully landed on her back so she could force her head underwater.

"Let go of me," Karah gurgled as she fought her way to the surface. "What are you trying to do, drown me?"

"You're not worth the trouble that would cause me," Gigo said as Karah's head came up for air and she grabbed a fistful of her hair. "I brought you here to teach you a lesson. You can't dismiss me. You can't transmute me out of your life."

"You're sick," Karah said as she went under again.

After a minute of wildly confused fighting a crocodile burst out of the water with nostrils pulsating like engine pistons. It wrapped around Gigo like a papoose and jackknifed taking her down. Karah couldn't see what was happening to Gigo underwater, but she was sure she was about to be the croc's second course. She swam hard and fast for shore hoping to escape. Gigo came catapulting out of the water and flew over her head beating her to the beach.

While Gigo limped into the woods with mud dripping from her ears, Karah heard the angry croc thrashing through the water toward her. She prayed she'd be as lucky and get spit out in one piece as the croc opened its jaw in her face. Once again Karah's prayers were answered. The croc didn't chomp down on her. It yelled: "What do you think you're doing?"

"Spot, is that you?" she said.

"Do you know any other crocodiles that would yell at you instead of eat you?" he said.

"I didn't recognize you without your jewels," she said as she dragged herself out of the water. "What happened to them?"

"Stop asking questions and tell me why you went swimming in the Archangels' Holy Prayer Garden Pond," he said.

"Their what?" Karah said. "Gigo told me it was a swimming pond and that it wasn't sacred."

"AND YOU BELIEVED HER?" he said.

Filled with despair Karah followed Spot and Progy through the woods on foot. She didn't feel like riding. The fun was gone from her day. Humiliation was setting in and she wasn't in a hurry knowing they were headed for Isabella's and Spot was only a warm up act compared to how she was going to react. When they arrived Progy parked himself in front of her cottage as Spot croced away. Sensing she needed to know he still loved her he turned and gave her a hug.

"Please come inside and help me explain why I did what I did," she said.

"There's no explanation that will change the truth."

"I know," she said. "I just need you to be there with me."

"I'm not a security blanket. It's time you started facing your issues on your own."

Karah took a moment to pray and ask God for forgiveness before walking into Isabella's kitchen. Hearing voices she tracked them to the library and listened with her ear pressed against the door. Her eyebrows rose and her lips parted when an unfamiliar voice impatiently said, "No, Isabella. I don't want another cup of tea. I want to know how long it's going to take Karah to get home." Chills went up her spine that caused her to take a backward step. The floor responded by creaking beneath her feet. Her hopes that no one heard were dashed when Isabella said, "Karah, stop eavesdropping and get in here." She walked in and stood before Isabella in patches of daylight creeping through lace eyelet curtains wondering who the forbidding woman was. She was relieved to see Corissa, Nony, and Jasmine, posed on the far side of the room.

"Karah, this is Ezer," Isabella said, increasing the tension in the room. "I believe I told you about her. Nony summoned her to report Gigo's duplicitous charade. She wants proof that you were led astray and unwittingly went swimming in the Archangels' Holy Prayer Garden Pond. She needs you to tell her why you did."

"Gigo told me it was a regular swimming pond that wasn't sacred," she said.

"AND YOU BELIEVED HER?" Isabella said.

Isabella's words banged on the walls as someone knocked on the front door. Corissa's cat sent a small rug sailing across the floor as it cleared out of the library. While Corissa left the room to see who was on the porch Karah wondered what spooked Whiskers. She stopped wondering when Corissa came back with Gigo and her shark-head father. She wished she, too, had a built in warning mechanism that would tell her when evil comes calling.

Gigo's father grabbed Gigo by the scruff of her neck and guardedly forced her to stand in the middle of the room.

Ezer walked up to her and said, "Isabella, tell me what I'm supposed to do with Gigo."

"I will," Isabella said. "I will be right back. I want to deal with Karah first. She should be past the point of falling for tricks."

Isabella turned Karah's cottage into a military compound and began her interrogation in front of Alexia whose brains were racing at full-speed from her part-time mirror throne. "What were you thinking?" she said. "Why haven't you learned who you can and can't trust? Why didn't you go straight to your training class and back home again the way you're supposed to? We'll have to finish this discussion later. I have to get back to dealing with Gigo. One more thing until then, you do have a built in warning mechanism that will tell you when evil is lurking behind a closed door. The Holy Spirit. It gives you discernment. You're not heeding the warnings. If something doesn't feel right don't do it," she said as she turned in her spiked heels and walked out.

Karah threw herself on her bed.

"My dear, I understand why Isabella is so upset," Alexia said, shaking her head. "You disobeyed her and we all know it was because you allowed your good senses to be overruled by tempting desires. You knew to not trust Gigo, but went along because of overconfidence in yourself and because she described something you wanted to see and do. You made up reasons to think it was okay. That's exactly what she hoped you'd do. You fell for her plot to tempt you into making a series of poor choices that could have had devastating consequences."

"So much for thinking I'm now infallible," Karah said. "I guess I'll always be a screwup. Who else but me is stupid enough to be lured to a swimming pond they only half-believed existed and by someone they only half-trusted. How dumb was that?"

"You're most certainly not dumb or stupid," Alexia said. "Satan is putting those thoughts in your head. He's trying to make you feel worse than you should so he can discourage you. You were listening to his suggestions when you went off with Gigo?"

"I was?" Karah said.

"Yes. Do you remember how you felt on the crooked path when the branch h-whacked you on the head and Progy had to dodge a falling rock? You sensed the need to turn around and go home, but you listened to Gigo when she dismissed your concerns. Satan was using her to lure you into trouble."

"Why didn't the Holy Spirit flatout tell me to go home," Karah said, "instead of only causing me to think I should?"

"God will not strong-arm you. The Holy Spirit sends suggestions. You have to choose to apply them to the choices before you. Chazz already explained this to you. It's rare for the Holy Spirit to directly say, 'No! Yes! Stop! Go! Don't do it! Turn around! Go home!' God wants His children to develop the habit of leaning into Him like you are right now so they can detect His still, small voice and choose to obey and follow His guidance without being told to.

"We all knew what was going to happen when you left Rabboni's office filled with pride and an overinflated sense of self-confidence because you won Round Two of *Get Out of the Underworld*. God allowed Gigo's plot to transpire so you'd find out what happens when you think, too, highly of yourself and don't listen for His guidance."

"I didn't know my feelings of dread were warning signals coming from God," Karah said.

"Well, now you do. Hopefully you'll remember what it feels like the next time you're in a questionable situation that makes you uncomfortable."

"Chazz told you this is how I roll," God interjected. "I'm all that's big, fast, and strong in your life. It's only because of My power that you can do anything. Do you promise to remember that?"

"Yes," Karah said as she filled with tearful remorse.

Chapter Fifteen

BEST AND WORST EVER!

THOUGH IT'D BEEN days since her altercation with Gigo in the Archangels' Holy Prayer Pond Karah still felt a sense of shame. She'd never gotten in so much trouble in one day by so many people in her life. Darkness ruled her mind by reminding her of how she'd failed. No one had been able to convince her she was smart and capable or that they'd only been upset because something terrible could have happened to her.

She didn't know what unconditional love was because she'd never experienced it. She walked toward Isabella's at dinnertime unable to stop thinking about how easy it was for Gigo to deceive her. She hesitated on the porch before going inside. When she peaked through the window and didn't see anyone she opened the door. As she did the house came alive with party guests shouting, "Happy Birthday," as they jumped from their hiding places.

"Make a wish and blow out your candles so you can open your

presents," Spike said as he ushered her to a pink birthday cake positioned under a cascade of balloons.

Karah excitedly kissed and hugged Isabella; squeezed Nony, Corissa, and Jasmine; cuddled Bettina; and stood before Rabboni honored that a man like Him cared enough about her to spend His valuable time attending a party for her. The sight of Chazz sucking ice cream out of the bottom of his cone and Stavvon holding a large gift bag earned them pecks on their cheeks. She marveled at the sight of her wonderful friends and quickly noticed Spot, Progy, and Aamir were absent.

"I'm sure they'll be here soon," Isabella said, sensing her disappointment.

"Open my present first," Spike said. "It's a set of flashcards of all the Angels and beings in Khalee."

"Thank you, Spike. Now I have names to go with all the faces," she said as she tore the wrapping paper.

"I wear these rings when I arrange the stars," Bettina said as she opened her jewelry box and held it out to Karah. "I brought them all so you could pick your favorite and have something of mine to keep close to you forever." Karah didn't look inside the box. She looked at the sapphire ring on Bettina's finger. Bettina noticed and immediately took it off. "This ring will grow as you grow," she said as she put it on Karah's finger and it shrank to fit.

Isabella made sure she was next and beamed as she entered the circle of fun. Karah's heart melted when she opened the ornate gift box Isabella handed her and saw a porcelain grand piano music box adorned with intricate pastel roses. She hushed her party guests when her favorite Chopin waltz began to play as she turned the gold winding mechanism on the bottom.

Thinking they'd been patient enough Stavvon and Chazz seized an opportunity to give Karah their presents and excitedly did the unwrapping for her by reaching into the bag simultaneously.

"Mine is the yellow sunflower," Chazz said. "The blue tulip is from Stavvon. They're phoneflowers. Now you can call us anytime you want. All you have to do is yell into the petals."

"We know you like pink," Stavvon said. "We wanted you to have phoneflowers in our favorite colors so you'd know which one of us you're calling."

"These are phones?" Karah said. "You have no idea how much I've missed having one."

"I do. I have sisters," Stavvon said as he walked her phoneflowers around the room so everyone could see them up close.

Rabboni was last. After the room quieted down He lifted a stunning present sitting on His lap and handed it to Karah. She admired the delicious bow twisting and twirling in ways she didn't think possible and saw a question printed on it: *What Is The Key To Life?* When she attempted to remove the bow everyone throughout Khalee heard: BONG! BONG! BONG! BONG! "What was that?" she said.

"There's an alarm connected to the bow," Rabboni said, trying not to smile. "When you can answer the question you'll be able to remove the bow and open your present."

"That means everyone in Khalee will know every time I get the answer wrong," she said.

"They will, won't they," He said with a sly wink. "That might make you try harder to get it right."

Rabboni wasn't the only one trying not to chuckle. They all knew she wanted her present open. They also knew she didn't want all of Khalee being kept apprised of her progress. Hoping she could test answers Karah thought of a response and barely touched the bow with her fingertip. The loud 'BONG! BONG! BONG! BONG!' sounded again. This time the room lost control. There was suddenly more, much welcomed, laughter filling Isabella's home than she'd experienced in many years.

"This is embarrassing," Karah said. "Now everyone knows I can't open my present."

"Only a gazillion spirits in the Kingdom," Nony said.

"They're going to think I'm an idiot," Karah said.

"Those kinds of thoughts come from Satan. He's trying to make you worry about what other people think," Rabboni said. "Stop listening to him. Don't be afraid of wrong answers they lead to correct answers."

"But an alarm?" she said.

"Yes, an alarm," He said, "so you can get used to testing your knowledge in the world. If you don't your mind will be limited."

"Is that how you got so smart?" she said.

"I was born knowing All," He said.

Tripping over themselves Spot, Progy, and Aamir came flopping and croaking and slithering through the door out of breath.

"You're late," Isabella said.

"Theee blacksmithhh gottt calleddd awayyy," Aamir said as Progy hopped into Karah's lap and handed her a little gift. "Weee haddd tooo gooo elsewhereee attt theee lasttt minuteee."

"Will an alarm go off if I try to open this?" Karah said, smiling at Rabboni.

"Whyyy woulddd ittt haveee annn alarmmm?" Aamir said.

"Never mind," Karah said while everyone laughed.

"Speaking of an alarm, did you hear all the BONGING going on?" Spot said. "What was that?"

"Ask Rabboni," Karah said as she ripped open her final gift.

Spot, Progy, and Aamir hovered around her as she pulled out a silver bracelet with three dangling charms: A little frog riding a bicycle, a tiny cobra curled around a stick, and a little lizard holding a camera. "I love it," she said. "But Spot, you're not a little lizard, you're a crocodile."

"For you I'll always be a little lizard," he said.

As Bettina helped Karah clasp her charm bracelet on her wrist the room suddenly became deadly quiet. Corissa froze with a cup of punch posed on her lips as Isabella rushed to her study. Rabboni signaled for Bettina, Progy, Spot, Aamir, Spike, Corissa, Nony, Jasmine, Stavvon, and Chazz to join Him in the kitchen. Karah followed and watched her entire God Squad dematerialize.

Concerned but also comforted by the fact that Isabella was still home she took her gifts to her cottage, put her pajamas on, and sat staring at the present with the bow everyone thought was so amusing. She thought of an answer. BONG! BONG! BONG! BONG! She thought of another answer. BONG! BONG! BONG! BONG! She thought of another, and then another, and another.

When all she got were BONGS bouncing off her cottage walls she turned to her window and peered across the garden. Seeing Isabella's candle burning gave her great pause. She hadn't seen it flaming since the night she'd arrived and was examined by it, but this time it wasn't changing colors. It started out green and stayed green. *"If green means go,"* she considered, *"who's supposed to go and where and why are they supposed to go wherever they're supposed to go?"* she put her robe on and headed for Isabella's study hoping to find out.

Arriving at the back door in time to unexpectedly intercept Corissa, Nony, and Jasmine as they came creeping around the side of the house she noticed Corissa trying to keep her weight off her right leg. "What happened? What's going on?" she said as birds flew out of a nearby bush. When no one answered she followed them to Jasmine's room. To her surprise Corissa started walking strong enough to run a race.

"I heard you didn't get Rabboni's present open while we were gone," Nony said.

"All the BONGING was unmistakable," Karah said.

"If you don't like 'All the BONGING' you should be studying to discover the answer," Jasmine said.

"I tried. I couldn't concentrate. I was worried about what was going on. Now I'm worried about Corissa. Why was she limping?"

"If you're supposed to know something you'll be told," Corissa said. "What goes on in Khalee isn't anything you need to worry about. You needn't worry about me either."

"Let's restart your birthday party," Jasmine said. "We can go outside and play *Get Out of the Underworld*. It will take your mind off things."

"We don't have a game board," Karah said.

"Make one," Corissa said, "while I get slices of your birthday cake."

While Nony and Jasmine caught different colored fireflies to use as playing pieces, Karah created the outline of a serpent with chocolate covered popcorn and inserted her birthday flashcards for spaces to land on. She collected fruit leaves to use as *Stand Up For Yourself Scripture Cards,* designated a spot in the grass as the entrance to the Underworld, and explained the rules.

When Corissa returned with plates of cake she handed them out and gave the fireflies a stay-in-one-place-if-you-want-to-play look.

"It's your birthday, Karah," Nony said. "You get to go first."

Karah stopped smiling as her firefly landed on Ezer knowing she was going to have to answer a 'Truth' question. "Thanks for letting me go first," she said.

After a hurried consultation Corissa, Nony, and Jasmine, came up with a question.

"Tell us something no one knows about you," Corissa said.

"That's impossible. Everyone in Khalee knows everything there is to know," Karah said.

"Not everyone," Jasmine said.

"Come on. I'm sure you can think of something," Nony said.

There was something, but there was a problem with the something. The something was a secret Isabella told her she couldn't tell.

"Tell us a truth," Corissa said.

Karah remained hesitant. It was tell what she wasn't supposed to tell or lie and get shipped to the Underworld - Game over. What a choice.

"One," Corissa said, holding up a finger.

Karah unfolded her lips but no words would come out.

"Two," Jasmine said, pointing two fingers at her.

"I can't," Karah said, desperately trying to think of something other than what she was thinking.

"Three," Nony said, raising three fingers.

"Okay. Okay," Karah said. "Queen Alexia carved herself into my mirror frame. She's staying in my cottage with me."

When firecrackers unexpectedly burst through the garden Karah leapt for the fruit bushes as Corissa, Nony, and Jasmine jumped to their feet.

"I heard everything. Karah's a liar!" Gigo said, running toward them with a firework detonation device in her hand. "There's no way Queen Alexia would establish a throne on her mirror."

Feeling like a criminal under fire Karah snapped. "You know what? Your name reminds me of something. Hummmmm. Let's see. Does G-I-G-O stand for Garbage-In-Garbage-Out?"

"Don't worry your pretty little pea-brain about what goes in and out of me," Gigo said as she snatched Corissa's cat off the ground and hurled it through the night air.

Isabella ran out her kitchen door in time to see Karah land on top of Gigo. Her timing was perfect in that respect, but not in another. One of Gigo's firecrackers had a delayed reaction. It exploded as she came into view and blew through the quilt in her hand setting it ablaze while Karah and Gigo wrestled on the ground. She rushed to the brawling girls, grabbed the back of Karah's pajama collar, and pulled her off Gigo with one hand while holding her burning quilt in the other.

"WHAT'S GOING ON?" she said.

"Karah told a lie," Gigo said as she jumped to her feet. "She said Queen Alexia is carved in her mirror frame and staying in her cottage with her. Queen Alexia would never do that. I'm going to get Ezer and tell her Karah is telling lies."

"You're not going anywhere," Isabella said as Karah tried to wiggle free and Gigo ran off.

Karah looked into the wild flames in Isabella's eyes wondering if the fruit bushes wilted at the sound of her voice. She closed her throat up tight to make sure she didn't say anything that might make her madder than she already was.

Corissa broke into long strides hurrying after Gigo.

Nony and Jasmine ran into the house and opened a window so they could watch and listen to Karah try to tunnel out of the trouble she'd gotten herself into. It had been a long time since they'd seen Isabella erupt.

"Gigo started it," Karah said as she hung twitching and flinching in Isabella's grip. "She threw Whiskers. Whiskers can't fly."

"Gigo is one thing. You're quite another," Isabella said. "I'm upset about you telling about Alexia and you know it. What got into you? How could you?"

"I didn't tell Gigo," Karah said. "She was hiding in the bushes listening. We were playing *Get Out of the Underworld*. I had to answer a truth question, tell the girls something they didn't already know about me or go to the Underworld."

"You sacrificed our trust in you, your reputation, and the special privilege Alexia gave you to avoid having to go into a fake Underworld hole you made in the grass?" Isabella said.

"It sounds horrible when you put it that way," Karah said.

"BECAUSE IT IS!" Isabella said.

"But Gigo did something horrible, too."

"Does that make it okay for you?"

"You made the same mistake when you told me about Alexia."

"Yes, I did. I made a mistake. You are also allowed to make mistakes, but you didn't make a mistake. You purposefully blabbed. My concern is the reason why. Were you filled with pride and feeling the need to brag?"

"I wouldn't do that."

"Then what possessed you?"

"They already know everything there is to know about me. I had to tell them something they didn't. What else could I have said?"

"You were playing a game. You didn't have to tell them anything. You could have told them to ask you a different question because the only thing they didn't know was something you promised not to tell. They would have respected your need and desire to not break a vow of secrecy. Besides, they already knew. They know Alexia is hanging out in your room when she's not needed elsewhere. You were being tested to see if you could put a sacred trust above self interest."

Karah didn't reply. She didn't need to. They both knew a razor-sharp point had been made and that one of them had felt the prick of it.

Chapter Sixteen

SHANGHAIED

A VERY, ASHAMED Karah sheepishly walked into her cottage with her eyes scanning the floor. When she mustered up the courage to apologize to Queen Alexia she discovered she'd vacated her throne. "Happy Birthday to me," she said as she flopped on her bed. She shuddered to think how Rabboni was going to react and the words: **'You're not expected to be perfect. You only need to keep trying to be the best you can be,'** came to mind. She covered her face with her hands wondering if God chimed in or if she was making excuses for herself.

She didn't even want to face Stavvon and Chazz. She ignored their phoneflower calls. Their hard knocks on her door also went unanswered, but that didn't stop them. They peeked through her window. When they saw her lying on her bed they climbed over the sill and walked slowly to her bedside knowing something was wrong.

"Did you hear us call you on your phoneflowers?" Stavvon said.

"Yes," Karah said.

"Well, why didn't you answer?" Chazz said.

"I didn't want to," she said.

"Why? What happened?" Stavvon said.

"Something awful," she said.

"Then it's a good thing we came over to take you out to finish your birthday celebration," Chazz said. "It will cheer you up."

"My birthday is quite over. It was already jump started once and I wish it hadn't been," she said.

"We get it," Stavvon said. "You got in trouble for something, but Chazz is right. Our plan will bring you out of this mood you're in."

"Nothing could cheer me up," she said. "I'm sickened by myself."

"Come on, Karah. This doesn't sound like you," Stavvon said. "Nothing could have happened that's that bad."

"You wanna bet?" she said as she leapt off her bed.

"All the more reason for you to go out. All the kids in Khalee go out for a midnight adventure in their pajamas on their thirteenth birthday," Chazz said. "We came to take you to see something."

"I don't want to go anywhere, especially in my pajamas," she said. "And you can't tempt me."

"But this is something you have to see," Stavvon said. "The hippos were turned into moonstones. They glow in the dark now."

"That's terrible," Karah said with growing interest.

"I know," Chazz said, "but they're not in any pain. The Chief Angels finished their investigation. We got to help."

"That's where we went when Rabboni *poofed* us out from under your balloons," Stavvon said.

"It's the perfect place to take you," Chazz said. "Someone has to take you out for your thirteenth birthday and that's us. Come on. We're not taking 'no' for an answer."

"You get to wear these special sunglasses so you can see in the dark," Stavvon said.

"They light up the night like the sun does the day," Chazz said.

"What are you going to use?" she said.

"We have power in our eyes now," Chazz said.

"I don't think I should go anywhere without asking," she said, staring at the magical glasses in Stavvon's hand, "and no one is talking to me. I think God gave up on me, too."

"That's not possible," Stavvon said. "He never gives up on anyone. No matter what."

"You're not supposed to ask for permission. That's not the way it works," Chazz said. "Thirteenth birthday adventures are shanghai escapades. Kids surprise kidnap each other out of bed and go out to do something fun."

"I'm sure Isabella is expecting it," Stavvon said. "She'll want to hear all about it in the morning."

Karah began to vacillate between thoughts of hippos mysteriously turning into glowing moonstones, a spectacular pair of sunglasses, and what she'd done to sorely disappoint Isabella.

"You have to come see them tonight," Chazz said. "They might transform back into hippos by morning."

"It might be the last bit of fun I have before Ezer comes for me," she considered with a heavy heart.

"It will put whatever happened out of your mind," Stavvon said. "I promise."

That did it. Karah put her coat on over her pajamas and slipped out the door behind Stavvon in her barefeet as he handed her the glasses she couldn't wait to put on.

Karah became alarmed when she began recognizing sights she'd seen during one of her walks with Isabella. "Stavvon are you sure this is the way?" she said. "Isabella told me to never go down this path."

"Don't worry, we're not going to take you over the border," he said.

"And just what's on the other side of the border?" she said, turning her sunglasses on him to light up his face.

"Satan's followers," Chazz said.

"You mean demons can walk in and out of Khalee?" she said.

"No," Stavvon said. "Beings can walk out and become demons but they can't walk back in. If they weren't allowed to leave, like the ones who left with Lucifer, they wouldn't be able to make the choice to stay and serve God."

"Who's Lucifer?" Karah said.

"Satan, the Devil, take your pick. Different names for one in the same," Stavvon said.

"Isabella was right. I don't want to go down this path," she said. "We should go back."

"You're with us," Chazz said. "We would never let you stumble out of Khalee."

"Besides, this is as far as we're going," Stavvon said. "You'll be able to see the hippo moonstones when we climb to the top of this rock wall."

"I have to climb? Why can't you blast me up there with the power you now have in your eyes?" she said.

"Because you'd explode," Chazz said.

"Can you at least catch me if I fall?" she said.

"If you don't land on our heads and take us down with you," Stavvon said. "Now stop talking and start climbing."

"This better be worth it," she said as she nudged her fingers and toes into slimy rock crevasses.

Karah gasped when she reached the edge of the cliff and saw what used to be hippos.

"Welcome to Moonstone Marsh," a moonstone said.

"I didn't know they could talk," Chazz said.

"They didn't talk to the Chief Angels," Stavvon said.

Karah looked wide-eyed at Stavvon and Chazz when it belched and the marsh rippled around it.

"You'd better get outta here," a baby moonstone in the middle said. "The Commander might come back and do to you what he did to me."

"Commander?" Karah said, thinking of her nightmare.

"Don't that beat all. She doesn't even know about the Commander," a snippy moonstone said.

"You said evil can't get into Khalee," Karah said, turning to Stavvon and Chazz.

"Only if God allows," Chazz said.

"Allow? Why would He allow that?" she said, pointing.

"If He did it was for a good reason," Stavvon said. "Nothing can happen that God doesn't know about and there's always a good reason for whatever He does allow - No matter what."

"You do know the Commander works for Satan, don't you?" a female moonstone said.

"Yes," Karah said. "Why did he do this to you?"

"Because we refused to help him get you out of Khalee," a moonstone next to her foot said.

"This happened because you were protecting me?" Karah said.

A sudden hurricane-force wind came from out of nowhere.

"Karah, we have to go," Chazz said. "Something bad is about to happen."

"No! We have to stay and help the hippos," she said.

"You help us?" a grumpy moonstone said. "Maybe you could kiss us and we'd all turn into Princes and Princesses. Come over here cutie, me first."

"Please go," a large moonstone said with the voice of authority. "He's only cranky because he got moonstoned."

"And you're not?" a moonstone in the back of the pack said.

"Which one of you is Helki?" Karah said.

"None of them. She was visiting another herd when this happened," Stavvon said. "Now, come on. Let's go. We have to get you out of here."

"I said I'm not leaving," Karah said.

"Stavvon is right. We have to go, right now," Chazz said as he grabbed her arm.

"I'm staying," Karah said as she freed herself from Chazz's grip. "I don't care if it's dangerous. I can't run away and hide in comfort and leave them like this. The hippos helped me. I have to do something to help them in return."

"What do you think you can do that the Chief Angels can't?" Chazz said. "We already told you there's a plan in place."

"What's the plan?" Karah said.

In that moment, the ground shook and split wide open between the scabbling friend's feet.

"This better be Route D Back to Khalee," Karah said as she tumbled into the abyss.

After landing with a thud one on top the other Stavvon crawled out from the bottom of the heap and lifted Karah's head.

"Is she dead?" Chazz said.

"I don't think so," Karah said. "I can hear you talking."

"Did the Commander capture us?" Chazz said.

"Him or Satan," Stavvon thought.

Karah jumped to her feet, straightened her sunglasses, and flattened herself against a dirt wall. When she felt something on her neck she turned around. Once illuminated she saw what her two capeless crusaders had already seen - Thousands of worms oozing out of the cracks. "Please tell me you can destroy those with your eyes?" she said as she jumped away from them.

"We can," Stavvon said.

"Then do it. Hurry," she said. "Some of them are about to pop out."

Stavvon and Chazz stared and stared at the worms imagining them bursting into flames, but nothing happened.

"We must not have any power down here," Chazz said.

"How does that explain why we can still see in the dark?" Stavvon said.

While Stavvon and Chazz consulted each other Karah spotted an army of skeletons marching toward them carrying searchlights and shrieked, "We're gonna die!"

Stavvon put his hand over her mouth to silence her as he flatten her against the worm wall to hide her. This time she didn't let out a sound when she felt worms on her neck. She let her face articulate her horror. Stavvon and Chazz also backed into the worms counting three freakish skeleton soldiers in a row and dozens of rows. They held their breath hoping they would go unnoticed, but each passing skeleton looked at them and opened its jaw and snapped it closed all without missing a foot beat.

A light following the skeletons showed off the sinister details of an underground valley filled with jagged rocks and bones. It didn't pass them by the way the skeletons did. It stopped and looked at them. When they saw eyebrows pounding like ocean waves and a mouth jabbering like a jackhammer they took off running. Didn't help. The ghastly bobblehead popped up in front of them no matter what direction they went.

They dove into a narrow cave thinking they were safe, but three bats followed them and clasped handcuffs around their wrists. Their bat-captors then flew around the underground valley with a screaming Karah and a freaked out Stavvon and Chazz dangling in their claws. Stavvon's shock turned to disbelief when he was lowered to the ground and a broom appeared in his hands as he was swished back and forth while suspended in midair. Chazz was equally perplexed when he was positioned in front of Stavvon with a scrub brush. Karah was horrified when she landed in front of the oozing wall of worms and a cloth appeared in her hand as a voice shouted, "Dust!"

"Dust those?" she said.

The three bats then began arguing with each other.

"Karah's too old?"

"No, she's not."

"Yes, she is."

"No, she isn't."

"Too old for what?" Karah said.

"A spanking," the bats simultaneously said.

When the worms started laughing the echoing affect was so loud Karah, Stavvon, and Chazz covered their ears. Their hands were still in place when they materialized on Isabella's porch before a crowd of spectators sipping tea and eating cookies. The three marauders' stark, white faces turned a deeply, embarrassed shade of red as they realized who was responsible for their downunder experience.

"Surprise!" Rabboni said as he appeared in Isabella's porch swing and stretched His legs out. "We also know how to pull-off a shanghai caper."

Stavvon and Chazz shamefully collapsed on the front steps reflecting on their fearful responses as Corissa, Nony, and Jasmine, scrambled out the front door.

"Were you in on this?" Karah said.

"We were the bats," Jasmine said.

"It was my idea to make you dust the worms," Nony said.

"Who was the jabber mouth?" Chazz said.

"Me," Isabella said.

"The marching skeletons were cool," Stavvon said.

"You want to go back and experience the real thing?" his father said.

"The skeletons were Spike's service staff," Corissa said. "He happily closed his café for the night so they could join in on the fun."

"Fun?" Karah said. "You call that fun? I can't believe you would do that to me. You really scared me. I thought we were gonners."

"Good!" Isabella said.

"Did you forget something?" Chazz said as he held his handcuffed wrists out.

"No," Isabella said. "I'm thinking about using them to dangle you from the rock wall you had Karah climb."

"What possessed you boys to take off with Karah in the middle of the night?" Stavvon's mother said.

"Same question for you, Missy," Isabella said.

"You want to know what possessed them?" Karah said.

"Don't play dumb with me," Isabella said. "You know exactly what I mean."

"It's not Karah's fault," Stavvon said. "I told her all kids in Khalee are shanghaied for a midnight adventure on their thirteenth birthday. I pushed her into going. She didn't want to."

"We both did," Chazz said.

"Boys, there's a world of difference between a thirteen-year-old Khaleean and a thirteen-year-old human. You know that," Isabella said.

"I'm in Khalee," Karah said.

"You didn't get here by dying," Isabella said. "Are you trying to make that happen? Your confidence is still going straight to your head. Now go to your cottage and stay there. You're no longer allowed to go anywhere without my permission." Isabella then stared at her captives' handcuffs and caused them to loosen and hit the ground with a clink, clank, clunk. "I did that even though every fiber in my being told me not to," she said.

Chapter Seventeen

SURRENDERED

"Did you enjoy your little trip to the Underworld?" Rabboni said as He lowered Himself into Karah's desk chair.

"You call that a little trip?" Karah said. "Were you down there, too?"

"I turned Spike and his café crew into the skeletons and the rock sediment into the worms you were so fond of," He said.

"Are you ever going to let me read your *Power of Imagination* book?" she said.

"No," He said.

"Can I make something materialize if I try hard and believe?" she said.

"No. It's your faith in God that moves Him to create things and plow down mountains for you. You're to rely solely on Him. His light. His word. You can't even take another breath unless it fits in with His plans for you. He gives talents and smarts and can quickly take them away. Anyone who thinks they're doing things on their own is mistaken.

When someone surrenders their desires and gifts God says, 'Okay, you're ready. I can now fly you over that mountain top and conquer the world for you.' Now, that's how to get things done!"

"Why did Satan turn against God?" Karah said as she pulled her Bible off a shelf. "How was it possible to get other Angels to follow him?"

"Satan was a beautiful and powerful Archangel. He became filled with pride and decided he didn't want to worship or serve God. He wanted to be God. God dispatched Isabella to send him to a place where he would suffer for eternity. To avenge himself he wants to destroy God's good and loving children like you. He doesn't want anyone to worship or serve God and live a blessed life. That's why he's determined to stop you from influencing children to follow God."

"God's powerful enough to stop him so why doesn't He?" she said.

"Someday He will. That time is not far off. For now Satan and his followers are allowed to try to manipulate humans so they'll have opportunities to choose to be obedient to God and not run astray under Satan's influence. He has unending grace and favor to offer all, but His abundant blessings are reserved for those who humbly surrender their life to His service.

"Surrendering takes great faith and courage. It's not for the fainthearted. It's not a cowardly cop-out response. Believers aren't dependent quitters and mature believers don't fret and cry and wring their hands when things get tough. They pray, look to God, and push through storms. They walk with Him through their hard times so they can get through their hard times.

"You were created in God's image. He has feelings and emotions just like you. He longs to abundantly bless all His children, but He can't. Do parents give their children gifts when they're lying, stealing, talking back, and skipping school, or worse?"

Karah shook her head.

"You're right. They don't because they can't reward bad decisions. It hurts God just as it hurts parents when they can't give their children the kinds of gifts they long to give them. It's not God's fault or a parent's fault when children lose rewards because they're behaving irresponsibly. It also hurts Him when His children stop believing in Him when He doesn't answer their prayers when their misbehaving activities are the reason He can't. Then there are those who lack the patience to wait for their prayers to be answered and take matters into their own hands."

"Why are people like that?" Karah said.

"Because they don't know God well enough to trust Him," Rabboni said. "When a believer gets to know God they can't help but trust Him and want to please Him. They want to do what's right and follow Him as best they can. The issue is most believers don't take the time to study the Bible so they can get to know Him and become His friend. They continue to live uninformed, lustful, greedy, impatient lives and are susceptible to Satan as a consequence. And that, my dear, is why God allows trials. He loves His children too much to protect them from experiences that will cause them to grow and draw near to Him."

"What will happen if I lack the courage to stand with God when I have to face Satan? I didn't do very, well tonight," Karah reflected.

"Let's talk about what will happen 'when' you do," Rabboni said. "You'll transform into a great warrior. God caused the moonstones to speak to you so you would know what happened to them. Your life was never meant to be about you. No one's is. You're to grow strong through life battles so you can help others. This time around you'll be fighting for your spiritual life and so the moonstoned hippos will turn back into happy hippos. You wanted to know what the plan is - You're it - You're the plan."

Karah dropped her forehead in her hands and said, "Will you stay and ask me *Get Out of the Underworld* questions?"

"Calm means what?" Rabboni said.

"Rabboni, are you ever afraid?" she said.

"Karah, in me there is no darkness," he said. "No fretters. Now let's stick with Me asking the questions and you answering them. Calm means what?"

"Stillness of heart and mind."

"Silence is where?"

"On the inside."

"How does one get silence?"

"By tuning out all distractions."

"What does it mean to follow God?"

"To obediently go and do whatever He tells you to go and do."

"Darkness is only darkness until what?"

"God shines the light of His word on it."

"Now can you answer the question on your birthday present bow?" Rabboni said.

Karah voiced an answer in her mind, attempted to remove the bow, and heard BONG! BONG! BONG! BONG! "I got all the other answers right," she said.

"Yes," Rabboni said. "Seems that scare you got tonight turned your mind on. Makes up for all the fuss you kids caused. Now, goodnight. There's a birthday present you need to study for."

Karah went face down on her Bible when Rabboni went *whoosh*. *"I'm going to have to do better than screech, "I'M GOING TO DIE," when something bad is about to happen,"* she told herself. She then pulled her oil lamp close so she could be closer to the light.

When Isabella saw Karah praying she flew through her cottage window and perched on her bedpost. Sensing her presence Karah lifted her head and said, "You were right to make me a prisoner in my bedroom."

"You're not a prisoner anywhere," Isabella said. "God wants you to know you're free wherever you are no matter what your circumstance. That's why He wants to take you on a trip with Him tonight. He wants to show you where you can go with Him from right where you are. He also has shanghai plans for you. After all, that is what friends do in Khalee. Isn't it? Capture and take each other on thirteenth birthday adventures."

Karah instantly fell into a deep sleep and saw someone following her. Like an affliction her desire to find out who it was wouldn't go away. When she turned toward the figure in the midst she found herself riding a horse bursting with rhythm and nobility. As the horse came to a halt on the edge of a bluff its eyes lit up a vast ocean flowing between two rocky shores. While staring at the wondrous sight she found herself sailing the waves on an hourglass and watching the sand turn into flowers as it sifted through the shapely bottle. Visions of her past then flickered through her mind and she instinctively realized she was coming of age as she drifted onto a sandy beach and saw ten teeny-tiny creatures with glowing wings.

"We're the Fruit Fairies. We're to instruct you on all of God's goodness that's supposed to abide in you," the chanting creatures chanted in unison. They then joined hands creating a circle around her and began sounding off their names:

"I'm Love."

"I'm Joy."

"I'm Peace."

"I'm Patience."

"I'm Kindness."

"I'm Goodness."

"I'm Faithfulness."

"I'm Gentleness."

"I'm Temperance."

"I'm Humility."

"You're the fruits I read about in Galatians," Karah said.

"Yes. Each of us represent a fruit of God's character. By our name you can tell which one," Gentleness said.

"You have to have all of us inside you to live a peaceful life," Peace said.

"All of you are supposed to be inside me at the same time," she said.

"Slow down. Don't jump to conclusions," Patience said. "Only all of what we represent."

"That's a relief," Karah said, "but I don't get Temperance. Oh, I'm sorry Temperance. I only meant I don't know what your name means."

"Don't worry, Karah," Temperance said. "I'm not offended."

"Would you have known what Temperance meant if Temperance had told you her name was Self-control?" Understanding said.

"Now, I get it," Karah said. "As in, I lacked Temperance when I lost control of my temper and hit Gigo because she threw Corissa's cat."

"Exactly," the Fruit Fairies said as one.

"You're soooo smart," Kindness said.

"Now it's time to celebrate," Joy said. "Start dancing. Dance. Dance.

Dance. Show how happy you are to be here. This is a great moment in your life."

Karah knew she was having a great moment, but couldn't think of a reason why she was supposed to be dancing.

"Think," Faithfulness said as she read Karah's perplexed look. "Do you remember the faithful Israelites who followed Moses into the desert? You're standing on that Holy Ground."

Karah looked down at her feet and saw a path flowing with swirls of milk and honey. Her body instantly burst into motion.

The Fruit Fairies blew kisses into the night air filling it with sparkling pink stars as they listened to joyous laughter rise from the center of her being. They then spoke in rehearsed chorus fashion bombarding her with a flood of statements:

"Bring sunshine to others. Do not quench God's Spirit. Examine everything carefully. Be watchful and ready to act but never hastily without listening for God's voice. Never let obstacles stop you - Ask God to deal with them. A person who bends is stronger than one who doesn't. Hold fast to all that's good because Satan, the theft, the father of all lies, will try to steal the fruits of your Spirit."

When the strum of a harp sounded Karah sadly watched her fairy friends flyaway. To her dismay the stars went with them heading for far away seas. She then witnessed horrors of the Underworld flash across the sky displaying visions of a burning road and birds bursting into flames.

Chapter Eighteen

THE EYES DID IT

TEN-MONTHS, FOUR-INCHES, AND six-additional-pounds after her unforgettable birthday party Karah sat at Isabella's desk thirstily reflecting upon all that had happened since she'd arrived in Khalee. Like it was yesterday she vividly recalled the garden variety brawl, getting sucked into a pretend Underworld, and going on a field trip with God. Harder for her to fathom was how secure she'd come to feel living in a secret community seemingly surrounded by evil wanting to destroy her.

The weight of living under Satan's radar still plagued her, but she'd grown beyond asking, 'Why can't I just be a painter or a pianist?' As much as she never ever wanted to face off with Satan she never ever wanted to leave Khalee and the creatures she'd come to love. There was no doubt in her mind, she knew she had hope for her life because of the Holy Trinity and the family of angelic citizens who treated her like a daughter and a little sister. They were her hope as much as she was the supposed future hope for children overwhelmed by evil influences on Earth.

Karah still didn't know how she was ever going to become a champion for others, but she'd learned she could take God at His word and that He equips His children with what they need to fulfill His purpose for them. Her first moment of possibility thinking came when Rabboni assured her God also assumes responsibility for ensuring His plans are accomplished. Him she trusted with absolute certainty. The person she didn't trust was herself because she knew her natural instincts had an overpowering ability to sprout up and mess things up.

Her attention returned to her Bible and she read the story about Joshua a fifth-time. The part about his army only having to faithfully walk around the city of Jericho believing God would supernaturally cause the walls to come tumbling down never ceased to amaze and encourage her. She got down on her knees and prayed: *"God please, please, please make it that easy for me. How about a dazzling one-eyed-wink that will make Satan go poof!"*

Hope flowed through her as she recalled how well she'd recently performed when Rabboni tested her to see how long it takes her mind to become orderly and peaceful while being threatening by scary things. The grand question, however, remained unanswered and her beautiful birthday gift unopened. It wasn't that she was slow. There were just, too, many possibilities as to what the answer might be. To some *'The Key to Life'* was to have a warm, loving family that knew how to love unconditionally - She considered that very reasonable, but knew it wasn't the answer. She knew she had to think her way to the answer because the thoughts leading to the answer were what would release the power in the answer. Despite her best efforts to stay awake her eyelids grew heavy and her Bible fell upon her chest like a blanket of protection as her right arm dropped to her side.

Isabella was not at all surprised when she found Karah asleep in her office. She knew her mind hadn't turned off the night before because she was excited about going to a Birthday Party for Jesus. She'd kept the Winter Carnival theme a secret. She couldn't wait for Karah to see the mechanical amusement park thrill rides and citizens clamoring up to cotton-candy carts and hotdog grills. She'd even planned a Snow Statue Sculpting Contest for the artisans.

When the SnowAngel appeared wanting to know if there was enough snow covering the ground Karah heard him talking to Isabella and woke up shouting, "Snow? It snowed?" she then thrusted herself at the window, raced out of the library, ran into her cottage, and shouted at Stavvon and Chazz through her phoneflowers telling them to come over right away for a snowball fight. While anxiously waiting for them she moved her curtains to one side and discovered Gigo peering through her window. Determined to challenge her and tell her to keep off Isabella's property she ran out the door.

Gigo took off swiftly dodging through trees making one difficult move after another. Unwilling to give up Karah followed her beyond the snow covered meadow and slid down the same mountain and landed in the same pile of brittle bugs. Having lost sight of her she jumped to her feet. When she located Gigo laughing at her from atop another hill she realized it was a mistake to have followed her. Infuriated with herself and Gigo, Karah glared at her wishing she could turn her into a gigantic pillar of salt until she heard the familiar sounds of squeaky wheels. Knowing it was her big, cuddly, bear-like friend her feet spun in the dirt. She went running for him as his wagon came barreling around a bend.

"Yas needs a rides?" Flapp said as he brought his tired, crabby horses to a stop.

"That's exactly what I need," Karah said. "Can you take me to Spike's Café? Everyone is meeting there for Jesus' Birthday Party. You can come. It's going to be starting soon."

"Wheres yas snakes friends?" he said.

"You don't have to worry about Aamir. He's in town at the party," she said as she climbed into the wagon.

"Thens lets goes littles ones," he said as he shook the horse's reins and smelled his armpits at the same time.

As her eyes crossed Karah spotted handcuffs dangling on his right hip. A sharp reminder he was in search of 'the tot with pigtails that comes with a reward.' She had two pigtails in plain view. *"He could have a lucid moment and realize I'm her. It's possible,"* she thought as she began inching herself away from him.

Karah was suddenly anxious to get out of the wagon, but not in the manner Gigo intended when she appeared in the road staring Flapp's galloping horses down with her percolating eyeballs. The astounded horses reared up as their eyes began spinning and raced wildly off carrying a stunned and scared driver and passenger with them.

Flapp remained solidly in the driver's seat. He was heavy enough to stay in one place. He also had a tight grip on the reins, not that it did any good. He had no control over his horses. They had no minds of their own after Gigo spooked them with her sinuous glare.

While the horses violently ran toward what Karah felt was certain disaster she struggled to hang on. To keep her safe Flapp shoved her into the back where she bounced around with his spices and olives. Knowing the wagon was no match for the speed or terrain Karah prepared to jump out until one harried turn caused the wagon to come unhitched from the horses and roll off a cliff leaving her no road to land on. As they were falling . . . falling . . . falling . . . falling . . . the deafening sounds of her screams and the smashing, shattering, and crashing of the wagon ended.

Karah pried her eyes open and was relieved to see Flapp smile even though it was forced. She picked her way through the wreckage as he reached for her until his eyes closed and he dissolved into the sand. Someone touched her back as she screamed, "FLAPP." She raised her right hand to block blinding rays of sun and saw a tall man under a hat with a narrow curved brim standing over her and desert between her and as far as she could see. "I'm outside of Khalee," she said. "The wagon fell out of Khalee. It rolled off a cliff."

"I know," the man said as he bent over and eerily bored a hole through her with his eyes.

Up close, Karah could see the demonic plastic disfigured face from her nightmare. Horrified, she scrambled to get away as he picked her up with his three-fingered and four-fingered hands.

"Shush," the Commander said as he flung her over his shoulder. "I'm going to take real good care of you."

It took some doing but the Commander managed to get her kicking feet and flailing arms tied up with a rope he found amongst the wagon pieces. He then searched his left pocket and pulled out an old stick of gum with the wrapper stuck to it like dried paint. Karah crinkled her nose when he held it out to her thinking it might be poisonous or that he might only be trying to be nice so he could try to brainwash her into crossing over to the evil side of life. She recalled Rabboni telling her how devious Satan's minions are. Determined to never become one of them she prayed for deliverance.

When the Commander picked her up and started walking away with her tucked under his arm she struggled inside the ropes and shouted, "Where are you taking me?"

"To a place that leads to the fiery gates of Hell," he said.

"God, do something," she screamed.

When Karah regained consciousness the Commander was walking through a street littered with creepy people. Lumps welled in her throat as evil beings gawked at her. She tightly closed her eyes to avoid a spotted, rabid jackal rocking in a chair outside a saloon and started praying again. Her hellish walk grew even more sickening when they passed teenage demons kicking a cat's head around in a playground near a rusted out swing set filled with little demonesses merrily cheering them on. The Commander then headed up the front steps of a broken-down house and said, "My Master will be here soon," as he walked through the front door.

Karah was temporarily relieved at the mention of the being's absence. It was a reprieve. Time to think. As she was set on her feet and the ropes used to bind her were loosed she fervently picked through her brain to devise an escape plan. She scanned the room noting it was nearly bare.

The only furnishings were a beat up table, two rickety chairs, and an old couch spitting stuffing out. There were no pictures. Only windows hung in the walls without the benefit of curtains to soften them. There wasn't even a rug in place to cover exposed splinters on the floor. She fixed her eyes on beads of condensation dripping down a glass of water the Commander handed her understanding why even a glass would cry in an evil master's shack.

Chapter Nineteen

MARKS OF THE DEVIL

"I GOT HER!" the Commander said as he hustled out the front door and onto the porch. Karah followed, but only as far as the window. From there she was horrified to see a woman who also had a plastic disfigured face that looked like it had caught on fire, melted, and hardened. She watched the woman put money in the Commander's hand and noticed she also had missing fingers. *"Marks of the Devil,"* she thought as she slid down the wall.

Realizing she had an unguarded chance to escape Karah ran searching for a back door. There wasn't one. Adding to her panic at every turn she only discovered stuck windows. A single wooden chair looked like an ideal window smashing tool, but she let it drop to the floor realizing breaking glass would draw their attention.

Praying the Commander and what was sure to be his Master would crawl back into the evil holes they emerged from she crept back to the front window to see if she could learn anything about their plans. When she heard the woman shout, "Where is she?" her fear took over. There being no place to hide she flung herself over the back of the couch and buried her face in the stinky cushions with terror swirling through her body.

"She's right there," the Commander said as he charged into the house like a stampeding bull.

"Where are her things?" his Master said as veins popped to the surface of her greasy forehead.

"I don't think she had any," he said.

"You don't think! Did you look around to make sure?" she said.

"No," the Commander said. "You only asked me to bring her."

"You idiot!" she said. "I wanted her and a special bracelet she isn't wearing. Take me to where you found her. I will help you search through her crash site."

"Now?" he said.

"Yes, now!" she said as she yanked the reward out of his hand. "Lock her up in the shed. If we find the bracelet you'll get your promised reward back."

Nervously following orders the Commander grabbed Karah and dragged her off the couch and across the floor like a rag doll. As he did the hair on the back of his Master's head parted revealing Maleeth, HIDEOUS IT's face.

"You are two-faced," Karah said, "just as Isabella said. You're a two-faced demoness. How could you let Satan turn you to the dark side?"

Maleeth smiled at Karah showing off her rotten teeth as she watched the Commander push her through the yard and into a wood hut and lock it.

"Be quiet," Maleeth said as Karah screamed for God and pounded on the door. "I, too, can hear from great distances. I'd better not hear one word out of you. You'll be sorry if I do," she said as she headed back to the house.

Desperate to get free Karah forgot all of what Rabboni had taught her. She rammed the door with her shoulder to see if she could break it down. It wouldn't budge. She rushed to a cabinet to look for tools she could use to pick at the hinges. There weren't any. She turned to a wall shelf. Using the shelves as a ladder she climbed to the top to look in the corners. Still no tools. Shaken and hurried she slipped and grabbed for a box to hold onto. As she and the box tumbled to the ground jigsaw puzzle pieces spilled out and began fitting themselves together in midair. She cried with relief when the swirling pieces created a live portrait of Queen Alexia. She excitedly grabbed it with both hands. In that instant, Maleeth's face appeared where Alexia's had been and her arms burst out of the picture and yanked Karah off her feet and into the picture - The portal to her Underworld chamber.

Queen Alexia urgently ordered Isabella and Ezer to be present while Flapp revealed Gigo's diabolical plot to get Karah out of Khalee. "Is mets thes ones withs thes eyes ons a dirts trails," he said as they appeared in chairs next to him. "Is tolds hers thes sames things Is dids Ms. Karahs. Thats Is was lookings fors a littles tots thats comes withs a rewards. Is thoughts a tots wus losts and needins tos bes returneds tos wheres hers belongs. Thes ones withs thes eyes tolds mes shes knews a tots whos wus takens aways froms hers familys. Hers tolds mes wheres and whens tos meets hers and thats shes brings hers tos mes. Thats alls Is dids. Is swears its. Is didnts knows its wus Ms. Karahs. Is was bringins Ms. Karahs tos a partys. Hers asks mes tos. Thats wheres wes wus goins whens wes runs intos thes ones withs thes eyes. Shes dids somethings withs thoses eyes a hers thats mades mes horses gos crazys. Is couldnts stops ems. Wes wents offs a cliffs and crasheds. Is don'ts knows whats happeneds afters thats."

Queen Alexia's Court knew God had given Gigo abundant space and grace and time and opportunities to make friends and get along or involve herself in Karah's demise. They were sorry she failed.

Ezer unswervingly set out to detain Gigo.

Isabella zapped herself to Jesus' office. Jesus raised His left hand to cause her to pause and remember they all knew it was to come to this for Karah and that God is in charge of all things.

Instant clamor was heard coming from the citizen's temple where every Angel, guardian being, and creature in Khalee was shoving their way inside singing: "Holy, Holy, Holy is the Lord God Almighty who was and is and forever will be Karah's source of hope and power."

Isabella transformed into her butterfly form to make her way through the crowd. It was a struggle to get everyone to quiet down, but when she lit and held up a candle they gave her their full attention. "God is Good! God is Great!" she proclaimed. "Karah, His little light will return. Our little one filled with bright-eyed eagerness will come back to us from the Underworld!"

Stavvon and Chazz weren't going to accept anything less. They ran out the back door. Jesus followed knowing they were going to slip into His office through an open window. He waited for them to come out knowing they would have His sacred book *The Power of Imagination* in hand. He transformed into an Eagle and soared to the secret snakehole entrance to the Underworld knowing it was their destination. Sitting in a tree He waited for them to arrive and watched closely as they jumped off their bikes and began thumbing through the book until they came to a passage about snakes. He also knew they would fail at trying to turn themselves into skinny-slippery-slitherers snaking their way into the Underworld, but let them keep trying until they started arguing about who was right and who was wrong. He flew out of the tree, snagged His book with His claws, and said, "Everything is in God's hands and that includes Karah. Now, get!"

Unwilling to give up Stavvon thought of something they could still do. They pedaled back to Town Square where they hid in a corner unfolding the details of a new and better plan. Once satisfied they ran to Jesus' office to discuss it with Him. When He didn't answer the door they opened it and went in. Chazz quickly located the *Get Out of the Underworld* game and a pair of infrared goggles for each warrior playing piece while Stavvon scribbled out their plan for Jesus and itemized what they were borrowing on a piece of paper. Moving on to stage two they went looking for SirVeyor. Upon seeing him walking toward the commissary they chased him down shouting, "SirVeyor will you please give us a set of blueprints of the Underworld?"

"Only if you take me with you," he said.

"Meet us at the ferry," Chazz said.

When they set their sites on the third key citizen they needed assistance from they pulled him aside to ask him if he would please change his next scheduled departure to the Underworld to 'NOW!' The Ferry Captain was agreeable until he looked over their shoulders and saw Jesus walking up behind them with SirVeyor, Corissa, Nony, Jasmine, Bettina, Spot, Progy, Aamir, and Spike in tow.

"Do I reprimand these WITs for conjuring up their own mission," Jesus said, "or let them proceed and turn this into an opportunity for them to demonstrate their military leadership skills?"

Sharing nods the Ferry Captain, SirVeyor, Corissa, Nony, Jasmine, Bettina, Spot, Progy, Aamir, and Spike raced each other to the ferry dock. They quickly boarded and settled into their seats as Chazz opened the *Get Out of the Underworld* game box so Karah's critter friends could climb out.

The Ferry pushed off from the dock as Stavvon explained their plan and asked SirVeyor to unfold his blueprint and point out every crooked corner, dark tunnel, and dimly lit hallway leading to Maleeth's and Satan's adjoining chambers. Stavvon and Chazz then looked at Jesus. Knowing just what to do He folded it into a one-inch square, squeezed it in His palm, released His fingers, and revealed a stack of thirty mini-maps of the Underworld.

When they quietly and slowly coasted into the Underworld Docking Station hoping to avoid detection Stavvon and Chazz quickly tucked a map into each critter's armor and whispered their instructions: "1) Slip into the Underworld. 2) Find Karah and give her hope. 3) Take no action on your own. 4) Report back as soon as possible." They then pulled two handfuls of little goggles with infrared lenses out of their pockets and enthusiastically fit and fastened them onto the heads of the excited little army that was willing to risk their lives by entering the Underworld so they could encourage TheirKarah.

Once ready the toy-sized KarahBrigade led by Jacinta proudly marched off the ferry in single file in front of Jesus and a hopeful crowd of Angels, guardians, and trainees. They then anxiously awaited their turn to take hold of a rope Chazz lowered into the snakehole so they could slide through the secret entrance.

Dangling below ground like a string of sausages they weren't a SWAT team or a group of Navy Seals or Ninjas on their way to save Karah. They were going to do what friends do - Make their presence known to remind her she was not alone. With their feet on top each other's shoulders they remained as still as possible awaiting orders. When Jacinta gave them the thumb-up-go signal they pulled their goggles down over their eyes, leapt off the rope, opened their maps, and quietly and carefully began traversing the dangerous corridors and passages.

The only sounds were those of deadly cockroaches they choked with their hands, cries from two-headed rats they smacked with their shields, and the groans of poisonous spiders they poked in the eyes with their knives and spears along the way.

Jacinta was relieved when she discovered nothing had changed since the Underworld's foundation had formed. Just as SirVeyor's blueprint indicated there were three left turns, then a right, then a left after the quarters that house Satan's headless ghouls and ghoulesses. She could see their target - Two side-by-side doors - Satan's and Maleeth's adjoining chambers. She also discovered a demonic guard dog in front of each door.

The DevilDogs spotted them and opened their fearsome jaws and quivering lips to expose their pointed, gnashing teeth, and dripping globs of slimy drool. Jacinta ordered her troop to do the same. "Return fire with your fearsome jaws and quivering lips. Expose your pointed, gnashing teeth, and dripping globs of slimy drool, and add hisssssssssing to the mix."

The battle was soon over. The frightened evil dogs slipped and fell on top each other while scampering away. Expecting an evil being to come rushing down the corridor to see what all the ruckus was about Jacinta ordered her petite patrol to back into the wall and freeze.

After a minute passed and no beings appeared Jacinta commanded her peeps to move in. Half lined up in front of a gaping crack under the left door. The other half lined up in front of an even larger crevice under the right door. Cringing at the thought of what was on the other side they jumped in and scrambled to get into place. In that moment, Maleeth walked out of Satan's chamber and stepped directly over one brigade of fifteen as they ducked. She then opened the door to her chamber and stepped on the crevasse hiding the other brigade of fifteen.

Jacinta popped her head out so her eyes could follow the heels of Maleeth's scabby feet. Her petite patrol followed suit. Their hearts sank when they spied Karah lying on an operating table.

Sensing an unexpected good presence Karah slowly turned her head and saw Jacinta bravely standing at the door and her troop's eyes peaking out of their foxhole. To protect their position she restrained from crying out to them, but she couldn't hold back her tears. Simply seeing her fearless little friends made her feel better. She was now not, so, alone.

Knowing their mission was accomplished and that it was time for Karah to seek God's presence and protection Jesus closed His eyes and communicated to Jacinta that she and her troop were to retreat.

Under protest Jacinta led the KarahBrigade back to where their escape rope was still dangling so Chazz could extract them. So disturbed by what she'd seen she tossed her night vision goggles on the ferry deck and lowered her chin as she climbed aboard.

"We can't leave Karah down there," Chazz said as he leapt out of his seat. "What if she freaks out as usual?"

"Karah isn't the one you need to have faith in," Corissa said.

"I want to get out and walk," Stavvon said. "I can't ride back to base in comfort while she's down there."

As Jesus nodded the ferry captain steered toward the bank of the river.

Chapter Twenty

FATHER OF ALL LIES AND LIARS

By the light of candles Karah could see Maleeth at her workbench clumsily arranging surgical tools. "What are you going to do with those?" she said.

"Don't worry. I'm not going to kill you. I wouldn't waste a perfectly good specimen," Maleeth said, approaching with a scalpel.

"*Specimen?*" Karah's mind spewed.

"Would you like to see my handiwork? Girls come in here. There's someone I'd like you to meet," she said with a beckoning smile.

Three zombies with translucent bodies floated through the wall wearing ragged scarves and dark circles around their pasty eyes. They mindlessly hovered and poked and prodded Karah as Maleeth maliciously played with her hair and ran a long, dirty fingernail across her cheek.

"God, do something. Stop them!" she said.

"Seriously? Do you really think God is going to help you? If He was,

WARRIORS OF THE LIGHT

He would have. Oh, look. Here you are, forgotten and all alone down here with me. Didn't you notice?" Maleeth said.

"I know God is going to deliver me from you! He's here with me right now!" Karah said. "I know it!"

"You're as dense as I thought. You being here means He's already washed His hands of you. You failed, too, many of His tests," Maleeth said.

"God promised to never abandon me," Karah said.

"Anyone would to escape your constant frenzied foolishness," Maleeth said. "If you join us we'll make you strong by zapping you. We won't make you go it alone the way He does."

"I'll never turn to the dark side," Karah said.

"This is the dark side?" Maleeth said. "They're the ones who have been lying to you."

"Who?" Karah said.

"Just every Angel, being, and creature in Khalee including Jesus," Maleeth said.

"They don't lie. They can't," Karah said.

"They can't?" Maleeth said. "Then how come you didn't meet Jesus the entire time you were in Khalee?"

"He was busy," Karah said.

"He was busy alright," Maleeth said. "Busy being Rabboni your Master Teacher. He posed as your private tutor for the past ten-months. You've been walking and talking and studying with the Son of God, Jesus Himself, and no one could tell you. Letting you think He was someone else was the same as lying to you."

"Why would they do such a thing?" Karah said.

"Because they don't trust you," Maleeth said.

"Why don't they trust me?" Karah said.

"You didn't give anyone a reason to think they could," Maleeth said. "How many times were you disobedient? A ton! You also broke vows and promises and couldn't keep your mouth shut about anything. You even blabbed about Alexia hanging out on your mirror."

"Who told you?" Karah said.

"The WITs you also mistakenly trust. They told me everything. There's a lot you don't know," Maleeth said.

The zombies flew off as Stavvon and Chazz were led across the room in shackles by a lumbering beast. Maleeth's cackle rose to a deafening level as her pet creature cut them loose and they stumbled and staggered into a corner. "These little liars were found loitering nearby. If you choose to join us I'll give you the power to decide their fates," she said.

The chains binding Karah's wrists and legs fell off as Maleeth lifted her hands. She jumped and ran to Stavvon and Chazz and fell to her knees in front of them with tears in her eyes. "Is it true? Am I finally hearing the truth?" she said.

"Isn't the fact that you're here proof enough that God decided to not save you?" Maleeth said. "He can only suffer so much failure from His children which is why you need my protection now."

"You can't tempt me with power or protection. Everything you said goes against what the Bible teaches," Karah said. "God is faithful. He loves and protects me even when I am frenzied and foolish. Nothing can pluck me from His hands."

"Wake up and look around, sweetness. You've done been plucked," Maleeth said.

"She's right," Stavvon said. "The Bible was written by men who only thought God was speaking to them."

"I can't believe you said that," Karah said. "You know that's not true. You don't sound like my Warriors in Training. Have you been brainwashed? You know the Bible is God breathed. You know He spoke to the prophets and apostles the way He speaks to us when He wants and needs to."

"You don't really believe God is still with you, either," Chazz said. "If you did you wouldn't have been terrified when the Commander found you and took you home with him. You were so scared you went running for doors and windows you could smash your way through."

"How would you know?" Karah said.

"You know we have power now," Stavvon said.

"I also know that you know it's impossible to be perfect. God and

Jesus are the only ones who are," Karah said. "They don't expect us to show Them how perfectly strong we are. They expect us to let Them show us how perfectly strong They are."

"That's the point. You didn't," Chazz said. "That's why you're here and that's the truth. I don't know why They decided to not come through for you. Maybe They changed Their minds about turning you into a spiritual warfare warrior."

"Maybe They were never sure about you to begin with," Stavvon said. "Maybe that's why no one was allowed to tell you Rabboni was really Jesus."

"We all know you would have treated Him like a rockstar the way you do Bettina," Chazz said.

"Why are you saying cruel and hurtful things to me?" Karah said. "You know I'm still learning. Aren't you the one's who taught me mission details are strictly withheld. Are you forgetting you didn't even know what Isabella looked like until I came along? You'd only seen a picture of her in her butterfly form. Only a few Khaleeans know what Queen Alexia looks like, yet she personally watched over me and even scolded me when Isabella was busy. If I wasn't supposed to know Jesus was Rabboni it had to be for a good reason. Angels appear in disguise on Earth all the time leaving humans wondering if they just met one. And so what if I think of Jesus as my favorite super hero - That's what He is to me. He's also my BFF!"

"But Karah, I thought I was your Robin?" Stavvon said.

"Now I know you're not my WITs," Karah said as she jumped to her feet with a finger pointed in their faces. She then turned on Maleeth and said, "One of your posers just blew a fuse or was working with a pathetic script. Stavvon is Batman and Chazz is his Robin."

"Your mind is sharp," Maleeth said as her Stavvon and Chazz imposters went up in flames. In that moment, the floor crumbled and Karah fell into a lower chamber along with the stones and rubble.

When the dust cleared, Karah found herself lying on a pillar sprouting up in the center of a ring of fire surrounded by soldiers with bent bows and fiery arrows. With pain shooting through her legs she raised herself onto her elbow and said, "God, why aren't you doing anything to help me?" When he didn't answer Karah fell silent thinking about everything Maleeth had said. *"What if I did already blow it? What if God did change His mind about me because I'm not perfect?"*

"Stop doubting and feeling sorry for yourself. Your fear and pity party is blocking My Spirit," God said in her mind.

"I'm trying," Karah said. "I can't do it. Please zap me and make me courageous and fearless."

"I won't do that. It's for your own good. You have to surrender your fears. You're here to experience what happens when you give them to me. Your mind stayed strong when you battled Maleeth that's why you outwitted her, but the war isn't over. You're still in Satan's grasp. Now be courageous and put your spiritual warfare armor on so you can stand strong with me and block Satan's evil from penetrating your brain."

When Karah quieted herself down a vision of her grandmother filled her mind. She watched her mix ingredients in a bowl on a counter. She watched her pour the batter into a pan filled with fruit and put the pan in an oven to bake. She heard her grandmother say, "Fully-baked cakes do not jiggle like Jell-O and they certainly don't melt like ice cream. Now get up!"

In that moment, Karah instinctively knew God allowed her to get sucked into the Underworld so He could use it as a fiery furnace to bake her and turn her into a warrior that wouldn't fall apart under pressure. *"This must be how bones turn into the Stand Up With God Kind,"* she mused.

"That's right, Karah. This is My refining process. Now put your spiritual warfare armor on so you can soar through this with Me."

"Soar through this?" Karah thought. She then did as she was told and began imagining different parts of God's protective armor. Beginning with a vision of her shirt turning into a breastplate she asked God to fill her with great courage and humble righteousness. Viewing her belt as God's belt of truth she asked Him to hold her mind together and strengthen it with the truth of His word. She looked at her shoes and asked Him to help her walk in His peace. She envisioned a helmet of salvation on her head and thanked Jesus for being her Savior and asked Him to guard her mind from fearful thoughts. She imagined a sword

in her hand and asked the Holy Spirit to bring every scripture to mind that would slice Satan into a gazillion pieces. She then held her hand out in front of her like a shield and asked God for the kind of faith that deflects Satan's fiery, poisonous arrows.

At the conclusion of her prayer and mental activity she was inexplicably able to rise and stand where moments before her body laid broken. She still felt pain, but didn't let it stop her. She grew strong and confident that an actual breastplate of courage was strapped to her chest for the world to see. She prepared to leap off the stone and over the ring of fire surrounding her. She didn't considered the distance. She didn't wonder what she would do once she was on the same side as the soldiers. She was completely unsure. She was only certain it was time to be a Daniel and surrender the results to God. She counted to three, discovered strength and courage she didn't know she had, and over she went.

The soldiers miraculously lowered their bows and arrows to let her pass.

"God, you are AWESOME!" Karah said as she headed for a flight of stairs.

Thwarting her escape Satan materialized as a spotted, rabid jackal blocking the stairwell.

Karah screamed and ran.

"You're not going anywhere," Satan said as he quickly transformed into his Handsome Prince of Darkness form in a black exquisitely tailored suit and grabbed her arm. "You're going to stay right here with me forever."

Forgetting to submit her fears to God, Karah shivered and sank under the scowl of his eyes and sinister smile.

When he saw how easily he terrified her Satan laughed wildly and forced her through an open door. "You my little Princess are a joke," he said as he prowled through his perverse chamber. "You aren't going to make it five minutes alone with me if you don't start making wise choices for a change and agree to stay. If you do I can and will give you great wealth and power. I can also make sure no harm ever comes to you."

"You can't tempt me. Your Hideous It henchwoman couldn't either," Karah said.

"Yes, Maleeth is rather hideous. Isn't she?" he said as he settled into a gold throne and crossed his legs.

"So are you," she said, taking backward steps.

"Thank you. I work hard at it," he said.

"I didn't mean it as a compliment," she said. "You're disgusting. You destroy people. I read about you in the Bible. I thought you'd have an odor. I was right. Your wicked smell hangs in the air."

"Ahhh, yes. There is a lovely scent in here, isn't there? The fragrance of the unfortunate I joyfully crushed in my hands," he said as he rose to his feet and began circling her. "But you're not so unfortunate, are you? You've become very fortunate since you were called by God, but that is also fortuitous for me. Because you're so precious to Him I will take my sweet time savoring your destruction with great pleasure."

"Who do you think you're sparring with?" God said as He caused a knock at the door to call Satan away and create a quiet moment in which to speak with Karah. "Gigo? Stop listening to him. He's toying with you and enjoying it. You can't debate him the way you did Maleeth. He's the Devil. He's no one to mess around with. You have to quote scripture. That's the only thing that works because My power is in it."

"Excuse the interruption," Satan said, like a fine and fancy gentleman as he returned wearing a suspicious look. "I was about to tell you what a special treat you are. I should thank God for letting me have you. If you could see yourself you'd know why I want to keep you around for entertainment purposes."

"I'm not your treat or your entertainment," Karah said.

"Oh, but you are. I find it thoroughly enjoyable to listen to you mouth-off and then watch you liquify into a mess right before my eyes. Does someone need to clean you up?" he said, raising his brows and licking his lips.

Knowing she'd once again resorted to brat-tactics and that she needed to stop-it Karah lowered her head to her knees and chanted: "I'm only going to focus on God. I'm only going to focus on God. I'm only going to focus on God. He caused the soldiers to freeze. He'll surely do something to stop Satan." She instantly felt strangely unafraid. She rose to her feet, straightened her back and her clothes, and bravely turned to face Satan.

"Bravo! Bravo! Take a bow!" Satan said as he clapped for her. "You're two-inches taller when you stand up straight. You're also prettier when you look me straight in the eye. I like it," he said as he walked toward her with a gleam in his eye.

"Get away from me," Karah said as she fell to her knees, shaking and praying.

"Talk to your Almighty God all you want. Won't do you any good. He's not as Great and Powerful as He claims. He couldn't even keep His hippos safe from my Commander," Satan said as he lifted her chin with his pointing finger.

Karah closed her eyes and remained silent.

"That's okay," he said as he backed away from her. "You don't have to tell me what you're thinking. I already know. I know because I've watched you respond in every situation you've ever been in. I know what makes you squirm and tick and what your fear and worry buttons are."

"Then you should already know that God is what 'literally' makes me tick," Karah said as she rose to her feet. "He said and it is written that I am a Holy vessel created for His purposes through which He will demonstrate the power of His grace, mercy, and riches before all men, women, and children."

"Stop quoting scripture! Your overconfidence in God is going to be your undoing. But just to show you how fair and reasonable I can be," he said, "I'm going to give you a choice. You can be turned into one of Maleeth's zombie girls or you can serve me."

"God said and it is written that I am to serve only Him," she said.

"You're a weak and hopeless failure. You don't have what it takes to serve God. Even if you did if you don't stay I will destroy someone else in your place. Take a look-see," he said.

A wall-sized plasma television transmitting visions of Isabella in hysterics appeared.

"Do you want to know why your beloved is incessantly crying?" he said.

Karah was paralyzed by the image and unable to speak.

Satan snapped his fingers and a different channel displayed ghouls in the Garden of the Heavenlies outside her house. "Your Isabella is upset because she's also my prisoner. I know how much you love her so I thought you should know I'm prepared to destroy her if you don't volunteer to stay with me. What's it going to be? My subjects are awaiting my orders. What do I tell them?"

"Tell them to go away and leave Isabella alone," she said. "She hasn't done anything to you. No one has."

"No one has done anything to me," Satan said. "Who do you think removed me from my position in Heaven? Who do you think is responsible?"

"You are," Karah said. "You brought that on yourself. Your pride and arrogance made you think you could be God. You even got some other Angels believing they could be like God. That was crazy! You had to be stopped. Isabella was only following God's instructions."

"I did what I did because I don't have to bow down to God," Satan said. "Now answer me. I'm only going to ask you one more time. Will you live your life for me if I leave Isabella alone?"

Realizing she was back to debating Satan instead of quoting scripture Karah turned inward to God and spoke out loud so Satan could hear. "God I thank you and praise You for Your promise to protect and deliver me from Satan. I know You'll protect Isabella, too. I take You at Your word. I'm also grateful that You let me have this experience because it's causing me to draw closer to You than ever before."

"SHUT UP!" Satan said, storming toward her.

Karah tossed Satan's words around in her mind and the Holy Spirit inspired her to unravel his lies and shout, "Away with you Satan. That's not Isabella in your fake movie. She doesn't cry like I do and if you could get to her you would have a long time ago. You also would have come for me at my cottage. You wouldn't have had to use Gigo to concoct a pitiful plan for me to crash and tumble my way out of Khalee. YOU ARE A LIAR AND THE FATHER OF ALL LIES AND LIARS."

"I TOLD YOU TO SHUT UP!" Satan said.

Karah looked him square in the eyes wondering if he was going to self-destruct.

"Maleeth get in here," Satan said. "This is your fault. I should never have let you toy with Karah before passing her on to me," he said as she materialized. "You should have gone up in flames with your pathetic imposters."

Karah filled with even more courage when Maleeth became smoke and ashes. The thrilling sensation of the Holy Spirit was racing through her veins and piercing Satan. She was now grateful for the mind-control games Jesus had her play that taught her how to let God take control. *"But I'm still clearly in the Underworld,"* she reminded herself. *"How am I going to get out and away from Satan? I have no weapons."*

She then promptly recalled the word transmuted - The word she thought was so horrible the first time she heard it - The word meaning darkness is transformed by light. It suddenly dawned on her. With great certainty she finally knew the answer that would open her birthday present. The one word answer to the question *What Is The Key To Life?* was LIGHT. She could see the bow unfurling itself.

She was now a Warrior - A beacon of God's LIGHT powered by His Holy Spirit. She became still and concentrated solely on God's LIGHT. She straightened her back, relaxed her shoulders, and raised her chin once again. This time her thoughts collided and completely pressed together filling her with courage. She was done baking. She flashed her blindingly bright eyes at Satan to show him her will. Her passion. Her determination. Her control. Her fearless strength – God's power and flooding LIGHT! *"The LIGHT of God's word was meant to change my life and change it has. LIGHT is the key to life,"* she mused.

Satan gasped. He'd never seen a human look into his eyes the way she was. The cold stare he'd received from his prisoner moments before had only been a preview of what he was now experiencing. He received her self-control with caution and closed his eyes to try to get her courageous stare out of his mind for his only source of power was the fear he could instill within her. But his arrogant disbelief caused him to reopen his eyes to see if she was truly and utterly surrendered to

God and unafraid of him. "This is preposterous," he said, upon seeing her eyes still brightly gleaming.

While she had Satan in an eyelock Karah fed him a dose of fruit by showing him a sincere, humble smile. His body began swelling like an inflatable beach ball. When she saw the affect she was having on him her smile stretched wider and her eyes grew brighter. As he was about to implode she remembered asking God to give her a dazzling one-eyed-wink that would cause him to go *poof*. Thinking she should give it a try she closed and opened one eye with a bling. It worked, but she was the one who went *poof!*

Chapter Twenty-One

STARKARAH

KARAH KNEW THE giant of a man standing before her with three-foot wide shoulders wearing flowing layers of white silk was the manifestation of God Himself. She wasn't surprised His face was aglow or that He had the presence of a rock. She was only surprised that His white shoulder length hair was wiry and not soft like clouds. She fell on her face before Him. A young male attendant appeared, lifted her by the hand, strapped a gold belt around her waist, and urgently said, "Cinch this up tight and hold on."

"Hold on? Why? What's going to happen now?" she said.

"That's the belt of truth," Isabella said as she appeared and God vanished. "Now you don't have to wear an imaginary one."

A look of wonder fell over Karah as she bolted into Isabella's arms. "I'm so ashamed of how I kept freaking out."

"But you kept trying," Jesus said as He materialized in a glowing

167

white robe. "You kept trying throughout your ordeal. You grew strong and transformed. You're now fully-baked and have what it takes to be a spiritual warfare warrior. You also have an incredible testimony to take back to Earth. Many won't believe you, but that's okay - Many didn't believe what I had to say either. There are people who think God is a little God and that He no longer works in ways you've experienced."

Karah fell to her knees sobbing. "I love you so much. Thank you for loving me and teaching me and taking care of me and not giving up on me so I could be of use to you. You make me feel wanted and needed."

"All of My children are wanted and needed," God said from afar, "that's why it's time for you to leave and go back to Earth where you can teach them how and why they need to draw close to Me."

"What? Just like that? Without warning? I have to leave?" Karah said.

"You know your place is on Earth," Jesus said, "where We can work Our real-magic through you. You knew the plan was for you to return."

"Earth is where you'll continue growing," Isabella said, "so you'll become even mightier than you already are. You have much to look forward to. I promise. More than you can possibly imagine."

"Like what?" Karah said.

"For starters you're getting a new mother. The kind you deserve. Do you remember telling me you wanted to be someone's daughter again?" Isabella said. "God said, 'It's done!' When He says, 'It's done!' - It's done! All you have to do is wait for that to transpire no matter how long it takes and no matter what happens in the meantime."

"You already know God is your true Daddy and that He's the biggest thing in any dark, scary valley. We can't tell you anything else," Jesus said. "You now have to walk-by-faith, step-by-step, day-by-day, trusting We only have good plans for you. Remember that the three of Us: God, your Father; God, the Son (Me, Jesus); and God, the Holy Ghost, are one. We All go where you go. There's no escaping Us so there truly is no reason for you to ever be fearful again."

"Karah, I already know every want, need, and desire you're ever going to have. You also need to know I will only do what is best for you. What might look and feel bad for a short or long while will turn into something

good and beautiful and bring you great favor and abundant blessing. Look what happened as a result of Maleeth being allowed to kidnap you - Horrifying turned into Hallelujah-look-at-Karah-now. You have one day to say your goodbyes."

"Only one?" Karah said.

"Yes, one! When I move I move quickly. Besides, more time isn't going to make your leaving any easier on you or anyone else. I will let Corissa, Nony, and Jasmine, stay until you go."

"There's something we would like to give you to make the separation easier," Jesus said as He opened His palms.

"I get to take the bracelet?" Karah said.

"Yes," Jesus said, "and all the memories you had while wearing it. It holds the jewels from one of My crowns."

"Who's ready for some fun?" Nony said as she appeared as the Angel of Truth and Justice carrying a measuring scale.

"I am Corissa," said as she materialized as the Angel of Strength and Courage wearing a skullcap crown and lion's mane.

"Me too," Jasmine said as she transformed into the Angel of Love and Understanding with jewels draped across her eyes.

"You're them," Karah said.

Karah's last day in Khalee was very difficult. Every room in Isabella's house turned into a place where mourners congregate after someone dies. Corissa, Nony, Jasmine, Spot, Progy, Aamir, Karah, Stavvon, and Chazz, tried to think of games they could play to distract themselves while Isabella created exotic desserts to lighten everyone's mood. The games and treats didn't work. Even Chazz's rendition of how he and Stavvon tried to turn themselves into skinny-slippery-slithering-snakes only provided a momentary diversion. When Spot had a sudden great idea he startled Isabella as she walked into her library with a commemorative invisible tray of root beer floats. She dropped them on the floor as he shouted, "Imagine all of us in bathing suits at Helki's hippo pond."

Poof! It was done.

The hippos rushed toward Karah so they'd get to be the one she'd ride upon. Helki resolved the debate within her ranks the way Isabella does in her's. She got her own way. She decided she would be the one to parade Karah through the tullies. She strutted toward her and knelt on one knee offering it as a step stool.

Karah was suddenly happy. She'd been so upset about leaving she'd forgot the hippos would be freed from Satan's hex if she won a spiritual warfare battle with him. With boundless enthusiasm she accepted Helki's bent knee and climbed aboard as Corissa, Nony, Jasmine, Spot, Progy, Aamir, Stavvon, and Chazz jumped on the backs of other hippos.

Isabella stood by watching and wishing she could stop time knowing Karah's going away party at Spike's had already started. She didn't want to interrupt everyone's fun so she imagined a solution. Stavvon and Chazz were suddenly wearing their dress white uniforms, Karah was sporting her favorite toga, and the hippos were sprouting wings and flying their special guests out of the marsh and off to Spike's while she changed into her butterfly form and landed on Karah's shoulder so she could ride along with her.

"Isabella, you do throw the best parties in the Universe," Karah said.

Karah had never seen so much *whooshing* and *zapping* going on as she did that day. For everyday before this day she had to do everything on her own. She now clearly understood why. She also understood why she was supposed to endure trials and count them as blessings, but that didn't mean she looked forward to having any even if she did have ready access to God and His special light force that could slay demons in the Underworld and on Earth.

When the hippos parked themselves at the curb their passengers saw nearly every Angel and creature in Khalee waiting in line for Spike to open his cafe doors. After the excitement of Karah's arrival it wasn't much of a party. No one wanted her to leave. Guests were quiet or silent. Food was served but no one ate. Even her bon-voyage cake was somberly plated and pushed aside.

Karah's mood fell hard. The ticking clock upon the wall made it impossible for her to enjoy herself. Knowing she wanted to go back to her cottage to wait out her final hour Isabella gave everyone a stay-put look when she rose to leave with Karah, Stavvon, and Chazz. Spot, Progy, and Aamir missed her cue. They followed so they could stop Karah outside on the sidewalk.

"Weee haveee goinggg awayyy presentsss forr youuu. Here'sss mineee," Aamir said as he handed her a charm in the shape of a mansion to add to her birthday bracelet. "You'lll needdd oneee offf theseee sooo weee cannn alll comeee forr sleepoversss attt theee sameee timeee."

"Move aside. It's my turn," Progy said as he presented a velvet drawstring bag. "It's another charm. You sitting behind a piano."

Spot was next. He pushed his way to Karah and handed her a lizard-shaped box. She smiled, kissed his nose, and pulled out an image of her holding a lizard, a cobra, and a frog.

Isabella turned to hide her tears and took Karah in hand when it seemed pointless for her to continue hugging her three guardian friends. She slowly walked away with her. Stavvon and Chazz quietly followed. There was no *poofing* or *whooshing* after that. Getting home was not something she was in a hurry to do for it was going to be the last time she would walk through Khalee with Karah.

When Karah could see her cottage she ran for it. Isabella motioned for Stavvon and Chazz to follow her. Unable and unwilling to say goodbye Stavvon and Chazz looked at each other and took off running in different directions. After composing herself Isabella walked into Karah's cottage and discovered her lying face down on her bed and Corissa, Nony, and Jasmine sitting on the floor with their heads in their hands.

The only thing that could shift anyone's attention was a knock at the door. Isabella's heart split open when she saw Bettina standing in the doorway. She was grateful God arranged for Karah's last moments in Khalee to be very, extra special.

"Karah, would you like to help me arrange the stars tonight?" Bettina said as she stepped inside.

Karah slowly nodded. It was what she always wanted, but she rightly sensed that Bettina had also been instructed to take her back to her orphanage. She got up without looking at anyone and started packing her backpack. The flashcards Spike gave her went into a zippered compartment. She carefully wrapped her magnificent porcelain grand piano music box in a cloth and placed it next to her phoneflowers. She paused when she noticed the message buds blinking. When she pressed the play buttons she heard Stavvon and Chazz shout, *"Call us when you get wherever it is you're going."*

She gravely resumed packing and picked up her birthday present from Jesus that came out of the box with the unnerving bow she would never forget - A canteen with a special cover that had bones attached to it. Bones to symbolize that she has *Stand Up With God Bones.* After attaching her canteen to her belt of truth she put her new charms on her bracelet and slipped her sapphire star ring on.

"Do you have everything?" Corissa said as she rose off the floor.

Karah nodded. Her bag was packed. What else was there left for her to do but go. She swiped at her tears as Corissa, Nony, and Jasmine group hugged her then burst out sobbing when Isabella reached for her. She wrapped her arms tightly around her waist not wanting to let go and swallowed hard and said, "You promise you'll come visit me?"

"We'll all watch over you," Queen Alexia said from her mirror throne as Isabella's face crumbled.

"All of us," Jasmine said as Bettina led her out the door.

In the most glorious place in all of Khalee with a majestic view of the Heavenly Kingdom Bettina positioned Karah by her side and handed her a starboard and starpen. She told her to draw on it and look up into the sky to see what would happen. After thinking a moment, Karah drew a picture that became a connect the star picture in the sky. She dotted the starboard with her star pen and watched more stars appear each time she did. She then wrote her name and watched it appear. As the Angels and beings in Khalee also saw her name in the sky they said, "We'll miss you, Karah." When she heard them she lowered her head and asked God if He would change His mind and let her stay. When

He didn't answer she wrote, "I'll miss you, too," and her reply appeared in the sky as her tears dripped onto the words she wrote.

"Now," Bettina said as she swabbed at her own eyes and nose, "we're going to create a star just for you. A star that everyone in Khalee will call *StarKarah*. It will come out every night. We'll look upon your star from Heaven while you look upon your star from Earth. What would you like your star to look like?"

"I want it to burst like the one you created when you put on a *StarWorksShow* for me the night I arrived at Isabella's," Karah said, looking into her eyes.

"Okay, then draw a big star on the starboard," Bettina said with tears dripping from her chin.

Karah did as Bettina instructed.

"Now create trails of stars shooting out of your big star and look into the sky," Bettina said.

Karah did and when she looked up she was riding her big star, *StarKarah*, heading for Earth with God's still, small, sweet voice whispering, **"Fly, My Sweetness,"** in her ear as she wondrously soared out of sight.

God created us to be with Him.
Our sins separate us from God.
Sins can not be removed by good deeds.
Paying the price for sin, Jesus died and rose again.
Everyone who trusts in Him alone has eternal life.
Your life with Jesus can start right now and last forever.

You can put your faith in Jesus right where you sit
and receive Him by reciting the following:

Dear God:

I believe! I believe and thank you for sending your Son to die in my place for my sins. I believe Jesus died on the cross for the sins of all mankind and rose again. I trust in Jesus and understand that it's my faith and belief in Jesus that will cause your spirit to supernaturally rise inside me. I receive your gift of eternal life through faith right now. Thank you for giving me the gift of living a new life with Jesus as my Lord and Savior. In Jesus' name, Amen.

Warriors Wanted
Apply Within
Matthew 5:16

C. E. JOHNSON
cejohnsontef@aol.com